A Killing at the Copa

Crime Fiction Inspired by the Music of Barry Manilow

Edited by J. Alan Hartman

White City

Press

A Killing at the Copa

Crime Fiction Inspired by the Music of Barry Manilow
Edited by J. Alan Hartman

This edition published by White City Press
An imprint of Misti Media LLC
https://whitecitypress.com
Available in both Paperback and eBook Editions
1 2 3 4 5 6 7 8 9 10
Copyright Respective Authors © 2025
Paperback ISBN: 9781963479706
eBook ISBN: 9781963479690

Acknowledgements

Sweet Life — Inspired by *Sweet Life* from the album *Barry Manilow* (1973)

Rain as Cold as Ice — Inspired by *Mandy* from the album *Barry Manilow II* (1974)

Radical Boys — Inspired by *Mandy* from the album *Barry Manilow II* (1974)

I Write the Songs — Inspired by *I Write the Songs* from the album *Tryin' to Get the Feeling* (1975)

The Daybreak Killer — Inspired by *Daybreak* from the album *This One's for You* (1976)

A Connecticut Stalker — Inspired by *Weekend in New England* from the album *This One's for You* (1976)

Can't Smile Without You — Inspired by *Can't Smile Without You* from the album *Even Now* (1978)

Ready to Take a Chance Again — Inspired by *Ready to Take a Chance Again* from the *Foul Play: Original Motion Picture Soundtrack* (1978)

Since You've Been Gone — Inspired by *Even Now* from the album *Even Now* (1978)

Bermuda Triangle — Inspired by *Bermuda Triangle* from the album *Barry* (1980)

Lonely Together — Inspired by *Lonely Together* from the album *Barry* (1980)

When the Sun Rises — Inspired by *Let's Take All Night (to Say Goodbye)* from the album *If I Should Love Again* (1981)

Some Kind of Friend — Inspired by *Some Kind of Friend* from the album *Here Comes the Night* (1982)

Getting Even Now — Inspired by *Even Now* from the album *Even Now* (1978)

Contents

Life With Barry

My sister, Lisa, and I spent the early years of our lives in a small town named Manlius. This suburb of Syracuse was the quintessential growing-up experience that comes to mind when you think of life in the early '70s: selling tomatoes from our garden at the end of the driveway in spring, drinking from the garden hose and catching fireflies in the summer, trick-or-treating around the neighborhood in plastic masks and flammable costumes in the fall and sledding down snowy hills in the winter.

We spent a lot of time in our basement, which was the main base for all our toys. Lisa had her Barbie Townhouse, Barbie Dream Camper and a very cool Barbie bathtub that could make soap bubbles. I had my Weebles Treehouse, Weebles Haunted Mansion, a yellow Tonka truck I'd ride around on, a cool little plastic bowling alley set that my friend Jared would break (and I haven't forgiven him for to this day) and books upon books. We would spend hours in the basement entertaining ourselves and each other. Lisa would play a huge part in teaching me reading and other subjects in full-on lessons she would create both on paper and tape recordings. Mind you, she also made "cracker soup" on her fake stove, mini-cakes in her Easy Bake Oven and convinced her gullible little brother to eat a brown crayon by telling me it was chocolate. Fun times.

Perhaps the biggest entertainment of all in that basement was music. We had a record player down there that was all ours. Mind you, Lisa's and my taste definitely differed. She was very much into Peter Frampton. Me? Barry Manilow.

I still can't tell you how I got interested in Barry (excuse me while I allow myself to be on a first name basis with him), except maybe because my mom was a fan too. Mom was really into music, and our

Sunday afternoon house cleaning sessions were full of Neil Diamond, Barbra Streisand, Kenny Rogers and Crystal Gayle on the 8-track player, a delightful "ca-chunk" being heard throughout the first floor of the house when the songs would change. Mom also encouraged our love for music. Any album we ever asked for we got. When one of Mom's friends suggested they take me to a Barry Manilow concert in Syracuse, she readily agreed. I don't remember much about that concert except for Barry coming on stage for "Copacabana," but I will always remember that I had a great time and it was my first concert ever. The only other experience that would come close would be when I saw Barry's musical *Copacabana* live in London many years later.

Lisa and I would stack up the albums on the record player so we could take turns. Barry's *Even Now* album side A would be followed by *Frampton Comes Alive* and then we'd flip the stack over to play the B sides. *Barry Manilow I, Barry Manilow II, Tryin' to Get the Feeling, This One's for You* and *Even Now* would all be in heavy rotation on my record player. Every good memory of those days is paired up with a Barry Manilow song.

We would move to Jacksonville, Florida at the beginning of the '80s and I often say this was the end of the childhood happiness I had known. Life would start to go downhill a bit from there. The parents got divorced, there were custody changes and remarriages, I would attend a total of three elementary schools, two middle schools and three high schools and never be in one long enough to make any lasting friendships. During these turbulent times I'd still turn to Barry for that bit of comfort. That soft voice with just a hint of New York to it. There was something reassuring about it.

Fast forward about 25 years and now I'm living in Las Vegas where Barry has a residency at the Westgate Las Vegas Casino and Resort. In fact, he's one of those rare entertainers that has signed a lifetime residency. He came out of the closet and married Garry Kief and they've been together since 1978. I came out years ago and married my husband Luis and, as I write this, we're days away from celebrating 20 years since we first met. Barry's had, well, some work done. I'm older and grayer.

I haven't been to see Barry yet at the Westgate, and I'm not sure what's holding me back. It might be not wanting to remember just how good those days were and how they turned so dark. It may be that I'm afraid to remember how much those songs mean to me and the emotional churn it might cause in my brain. Or, it may be that I want to keep those fleeting memories of a little boy in Syracuse, staring at a stage at a man wearing all white as he is pulled onto stage singing about Lola and Rico and Tony.

This anthology is a love letter to Barry and everything he's meant to me over the years. It's obviously inspired by the crime at the center of his song "Copacabana," but each of these authors delivers a new way of looking at the timelessness of Barry's music in a new light. For all the love and light in his songs, you can also find a little bit of darkness. The contributors have all found a way to reimagine Barry's songs into Something Else.

I recommend reading these stories with your favorite Barry album playing softly in the background. As for me, with the heavy lifting done of putting the anthology together, I'm going to retire to the couch with this anthology on my tablet, "Could It Be Magic" on my headphones and my brain taking me back to a moment in time of Lisa and I filled with happiness in a basement just outside of Syracuse.

J. Alan Hartman
February 2025

Sweet Life

Inspired by *Sweet Life* from the album
Barry Manilow (1973)

Karen Keeley

Greta was out of the office, a doctor's appointment, according to the calendar on her desk, which left me to my own devices, spending time with the crossword in the daily newspaper, puzzled by the clue, 'the proverbial proud bird,' seven letters, when Roberta Suiter, Bobbi to her friends, walked in.

A week earlier, Bobbi and I had an impromptu dinner, she certain I was not feeding myself properly. We'd bumped into each other at the green grocer's over on Whitney where she worked part-time, me scouting out the cabbage, lettuce and asparagus because Greta had been on my case about not eating enough greens. According to her, I needed more fiber in my diet. I'd accepted Bobbi's invite, and helped myself to a hearty portion of chicken fricassee with dumplings along with a slice of peach cobbler, a six-pack of Bud Light the chaser, shared between the two of us. As to the cleaning up, she told me not to worry, she'd tackle the dishes in the morning. I'd taken myself home, thoroughly satisfied.

Bobbi and I first met in grade school, our houses side by side on the same street, maybe three blocks from the Shubert Theatre over on College Drive. It was there Bobbi and I each had our first kiss, not with each other, thank Christ, remaining good buddies throughout middle school and beyond. She'd always said what I lacked in physique, I made up for in personality which had cemented our friendship.

Following graduation, she married Hank Suiter, a good kisser right out of the gate, according to Bobbi, no kids, but that didn't stop her from volunteering her time to organize church picnics or fussing over the mutts at the SPCA when not working her day job.

Most everyone in the neighborhood knew Bobbi, a woman known for her peaceful disposition. But peace wasn't about to unfold this day.

She looked to be on the warpath, her clothes disheveled, some old housedress from some church rummage sale, a tattered cardigan, the sleeves shoved up to her elbows. Her handbag swung from her left arm, no makeup, no jewelry except for her wedding ring. Despite Hank's untimely death, she still wore the ring, telling anyone who cared to listen, she'd married the man of her dreams.

As for Hank, his dreams were cut short on a Thursday night, eight years ago, one of those freak accidents, according to law enforcement. A load of rebar torpedoed off the trailer of an eighteen-wheeler, three of the deadly missiles smashing through Hank's windshield, practically beheading the man. Not a pretty picture.

"Son of a biscuit, Peter Lockwood," she exclaimed, leaning over and grabbing her knees, obviously out of breath. If she'd run the six blocks from home, she was in better shape than I.

"You must come—now! There's been a murder."

I closed the section of the newspaper with the crossword, shoved the paper to one corner of my desk, lit up a cigarette. "I'm just peachy, Bobbi. How about you?"

"Don't be flippant," she snapped. "Didn't you hear me? There's been a murder."

"I would think law enforcement is all over it like white on rice. Why come to me?"

"Because you know her—knew her. Diana Gilbert, she's dead."

Diana, dead? Our homeroom teacher from middle school all those years ago? I didn't even know the woman was still alive much less in town. She'd skedaddled for parts unknown after the scandal which ruined her teaching career, accused of making whoopee with a sixteen-year-old, a fella who stood six foot two in his stocking feet, broad shoulders, with a swagger in his step, known to favor leather jackets and cowboy boots.

That too, had not been pretty.

At the time, those of us in her class, believed she was engaged, her fiancé drafted into the military, some plebe embroiled in the rigors of bootcamp, soon to be winging his way to Korea on a C-54 Skymaster. Bobbi and I were thirteen at the time. What did we care about Korea? Or the army, or malicious gossip? We only cared about Diana, our sun goddess, oh, she of the golden hair.

I stubbed out the half-finished cigarette, sparks flying. "When, where, how?"

"Come, I'll show you," said Bobbi.

With that, she turned, and scurried out of the office. I followed, having seized my fedora from the coat rack, wondering when Diana had returned to New Haven. She must be somewhere in her forties, a good ten years older than us. Where was she all these years? And why murder?

* * *

Thirty minutes later, I fiddled with a twig taken from the beaten path, Bobbi and I working our way toward the crime scene, using the twig to scrape the mud from the heels of my platform shoes. "This walk in the park isn't helping, Bobbi."

I'd spent a fortune on my shoes along with the high-waisted pants with the wide legs, turtlenecks and sweater vests, my signature look meant to convey credibility as a private eye. If anyone were to ask with a snarl, "How's that workin' for ya," right then, I'd have plugged them in the kisser.

Prior to our arrival, Bobbi had me go north on Whitney, then make a right on Cold Spring, my little VW bug laboring with the effort, which eventually took us to the southwest corner of East Rock Park, to a spot near the Mill River. It appeared to have flooded its banks due to all the rain we'd had, the area muddy, much like my muddy disposition.

We skirted the crime scene tape and found ourselves skulking about like a couple of would-be thieves, maybe a half mile back to the road. Bobbi shushed me, fingers held to her pursed lips. We then crept up on the site.

Detective Corrigan was there, a big man, bald up front, sporting a belly two sizes too large for his britches, his NYPD belt buckle buried in the flesh of his rotund stomach, the buckle a knockoff he'd found at a local pawn shop. His suit, shiny at the knees, had definitely seen better days. His tie, too.

He was a man not thrilled with the mud. "Christ," he bellowed. "Someone get me a pair of galoshes."

I figured it was too late for that.

"You can come on out, Lockwood. I see you there, hiding behind that tree."

Okay, so we were busted—Bobbi and I.

We broke cover, trotted on over to Corrigan.

"Why are you here? You know the victim?"

"We do," said Bobbi. "We did. Years ago. She was our school teacher."

Corrigan scratched a bushy eyebrow. "And I need to know this why?"

Bobbi looked at me, nodded in the affirmative, go for it.

"She left town under a dark cloud," I told him. "You might've heard of it."

"Sure, I heard of it," Corrigan snarled. "I can read, can't I? I looked through a couple of reports on the drive over."

"Who ID the body?" I asked, noticing a bunch of looky-loos had followed us in, most whispering amongst themselves, wondering what in blazes had happened.

Corrigan shouted at one of his guys to back 'em up, to get 'em well behind the crime scene tape. A couple of reporters were hollering for access, so far denied.

"Her husband," Corrigan said, jerking his chin to the left. There, sitting cross-legged on the ground was a bedraggled individual, him too, with mud on his shoes, mud on his trousers, mud on his hands, guilt in his eyes. If not for the blood he could've been another curious bystander taking a load off.

"He do the deed?" I asked.

Corrigan shook his head. "According to him, he found her. His name is Paul Sunderland. They were married sixteen years. He's feeling guilty 'coz he was unable to save her."

Corrigan took a stick of gum from his breast pocket, unwrapped it, tossed the gum in his mouth. Bobbi was shivering, not the least concerned about the gum nor the man. She'd done her duty, showed me the crime scene and now she wanted to leave.

"A couple of dogwalkers spotted him," Corrigan told us. "Cradling his wife's dead body. It was them who called it in."

"A likely murder?" asked Bobbi, unable to take her eyes from Diana's corpse despite her need to flee the scene.

As for the husband grieving over his dead wife, he'd taken no notice of Bobbi nor I, wringing his hands, bemoaning the fact his wife had been brutally killed, whining like some toddler cheated out of a sweetie or forced to eat the dreaded lima beans.

The medical examiner then arrived, a fussy little guy wearing bifocals and a three-piece suit, a conservative dark tie. He'd found a pair of gumboots, lucky him.

"A suspicious death," stated Corrigan. "Until the doc there says otherwise. She's been clobbered good and hard. We found the rock tossed into the bushes. Blood and hairs."

"Fingerprints?" I asked.

"Not likely," said Corrigan. "A weapon of convenience, by the look of it."

I nodded in agreement, taking a gander at Diana Gilbert, now Diana Sunderland. From what I could tell, boot prints had been trampled all over the crime scene which would make it difficult to tell who'd been with Diana, and who arrived later. Nothing helpful there.

I leaned into Bobbi, gave her a whisper. "There's bupkis to be had. Time to depart, dear lady." I turned to leave. She followed.

We were half way back to the car, pushing our way through the foliage, when she stated matter-of-fact, "I need you to find her killer, Peter. I'll hire you. I have some money left from Hank's life insurance policy."

"You'll do nothing of the sort," I countered. "It's a police matter."

"They'll be barking up the wrong tree," she said. "Some random attack in the park. I know what happened. But I need you to help me prove it."

* * *

Back at my office, a stiff drink of bourbon poured for each of us, Bobbi plopped onto the chair across from my desk, thoroughly dejected. She'd set her handbag on the floor beside her and pulled her arms free from that ratty old cardigan, tossing it onto the file cabinet. "Remember I told you about that concert I went to in New York?" she said.

"Which one?" I asked.

"Barry Manilow, last June. It was that Schaefer music festival in Central Park."

"Vaguely," I responded, tapping a cigarette from the package I religiously kept on my desk. I lit up, inhaled while tossing the spent match into the ashtray.

There was no sign of Greta. Maybe she'd gone to the bank after that doctor's appointment, or the hairdressers. Our office, not far from the Richard C. Lee Courthouse gave Greta handy access to the post office when needed. She'd been with me three years, very much my go-to gal, handy with a typewriter. Because of her, we operated like a well-oiled machine.

Bobbi appeared lost in thought when finally, she spoke. "I was in the Big Apple, the week of my birthday, visiting my cousin. She had a dentist appointment that Thursday so I took myself to Central Park. Of all people to be standing next to me in the crowd, it was Diana Gilbert. We were shoved in close, like sardines, hotter than hell too, what with the humidity."

"Never mind the humidity. What happened?" I asked.

"I recognized her right away," said Bobbi. "Twenty years older,

6

different hairstyle but still that gorgeous blonde, smooth and silky."

I nodded, an indication to continue.

"Barry was singing, 'Sweet Life,' the first I'd heard of him, seen him. I thought he was just swell. I remember thinking, he's gonna rocket into stardom."

"Good for you, and for Barry," I said. "What about Diana?"

"She and her husband were arguing. I didn't know he was the husband until later, but at any rate, there he was shout-whispering at her, looming over her like some vulture. Anyone standing near them couldn't help but overhear, his anger palpable. He wanted to leave. She didn't. Finally, he stormed off, pushing his way through the crowd. That left Diana standing beside me. That's when I said hello, told her who I was."

Bobbi inhaled, the memories obviously rushing in. "She burst into tears, grabbed my arm for support, and whispered, 'oh, sweet Bobbi. Of course, I remember you.' Well, that surprised me, as you can imagine. One thing led to another, and we ended up at some café somewhere on Park Avenue, the Upper East Side, drinking coffee and eating a Danish."

"A Danish. Of all the great food in New York, you pick a Danish."

"It was convenient," said Bobbi. "I don't remember the name of the café. Diana said she lived near there but she didn't want to go home. Not just yet. She told me about her life. After leaving New Haven, she changed her name, fell into a well of depression, struggled to get upright and mobile again. She finally managed a modicum of success through sheer determination. She married her fiancé a couple of years later, after his return from Korea."

Bobbi was twirling her glass, ice-cubes tinkling. I offered a refill which she accepted.

That pleasantry done, she told me, "Diana said no one in New York knew about the scandal which meant, she believed she'd made a clean break of it."

According to Bobbi, her husband wanted kids but they'd had no luck on getting pregnant. Paul blamed himself which changed him. He focused his time and attention on his career, alienating her, treating her as if she had no more importance than a family pet.

"And you think he killed her," I said.

Bobbi nodded. "Who else would it be? She came back and he followed her."

Yeah, it certainly appeared that way. Our bustling community of New Haven known for Yale University was a big draw for the academic types. But it wasn't all intellect and scholarly pursuits. There were those of us on the sidelines who enjoyed sports, cheering at football games when the weather cooperated. We hadn't had much cheer the past few weeks, lots of rain culminating in all that mud.

"Like I told you earlier, the police are on it," I said.

"Not all of it," said Bobbi. "What you don't know. It was all malicious lies, the accusations made against her. She'd tried to be something of a guidance counselor to a struggling student, him with failing grades, a rotten homelife. The kid got the wrong idea. To be run out of town, labeled a sexual predator—imagine the shame, the humiliation. That led to self-medicating, the pills and the booze. One night, she had a one-off with some fellow she met at a bar, feeling sorry for herself. That mistake resulted in her getting pregnant. Now what to do?"

Bobbi sat back and took in a bushel of air. "It was a difficult birth, all kinds of complications, the reason she couldn't have kids, something she didn't tell Paul, letting him believe he'd been the one shooting blanks."

"Hell of a descriptor, Bobbi."

She ignored me. "As for the baby's biological father, Diana didn't even have a name. If not for the Catholic diocese, she'd've been up the proverbial creek. No family, no friends, a woman totally alone. Nine months later she had the baby and put him up for adoption."

"You think Diana came back," I said. "Looking to find that baby. He'd be what? Seventeen, eighteen, by now, probably in high school himself, if we do the math."

Bobbi nodded. "Paul followed her, and killed her. Maybe he discovered the truth, a baby born out of wedlock, a complicated birth, Diana unable to conceive, ruining his chances at fatherhood. He'd been lied to."

I then offered my theory. "Maybe the child did it. Didn't want anything to do with Diana."

"Babies don't kill their mothers," she said.

"Some do. We read about it all the time in the papers, the tabloids. Or maybe it was the biological father. He knew about the pregnancy despite what Diana told you."

I'd finished my drink, set the glass on my desk. "It's now the seventies, Bobbi—we've no idea what happened to him. Maybe he kept tabs on Diana. How would she know?"

Bobbi shook her head, dismissing that train of thought. "Diana believed someone in New Haven adopted the child."

"Getting those records could be tough," I told her.

"But if anyone can do it, you can," said Bobbi. "Jackson Heights, that's where she was."

I smiled. "Your faith is reassuring." I squashed my half-finished smoke in the ashtray, fiddled with a paperclip. "I'll see what I can do."

"She deserved a sweet life," said Bobbi. "Just like Barry Manilow sang that day. You didn't hear him. It was special. The kind of song to give you hope. And Diana had hope. She'd lived with the guilt, the overwhelming sense of shame all these years, that one-night stand, forced to give her baby up for adoption, lying to her husband. She didn't deserve to die, no matter the sins of her past."

"According to you," I said. "But, my dear Bobbi, you must remember, you see the good in everybody. Even me."

* * *

A day later, I headed to the Big Apple, shifting gears on my little VW bug, driving south, enjoying the scenery. A sweet life as Bobbi would've said. And business was good, especially after Greta came on board.

Small jobs throughout the tri-state area consisting of finding lost articles, missing relatives, or simply validating witness statements tied to an upcoming court case. Other work included digging into allegations of fraud, embezzlement or outright theft, sharing the evidence with Corrigan and others like him, all of which kept me in the private eye business.

As I got closer to the city, the impressive skyline loomed large, concrete and glass, bridges and tunnels. Depending on the elevation, I sometimes caught a glimpse of the Empire State building, always an impressive sight which left me thinking about the many times Bobbi and I took in a movie at the ol' Shubert, sharing toffee and a big bucket of popcorn.

I eventually made my way into Jackson Heights and met with the Mother Superior, a large woman, a tad arthritic judging by the way she favored her left hip, walking with something of a limp as she led me back down the hallway toward her office. That affliction didn't seem to mess with her sunny disposition which left me with a sliver of hope.

"Our adoption records are sealed," she told me flat out, smiling her Madonna like smile. "As to the women in our care, it was all done through the seal of confession. They each made peace with their past sins."

"I get that," I said. "And thank you for seeing me. But couldn't you make an exception?"

I leaned back in my chair, crossed my ankles, clasped my hands in a virtuous rendition of prayer. "A woman has been brutally murdered, someone who was in your care. Diana Sunderland. Possibly Diana Gilbert when she was with you. Or, she may have used an alias. An anagram of her name."

I was thinking of those crossword puzzles I liked so well. I offered up the name Tina Dalbrige, it coming to me in a flash of creative intellect. That seemed to strike a chord.

The Mother Superior's eyes darkened, some cloud of memory bubbling up. She wasn't sure what to do with that. "Facts don't change just because you wish them to, Mr. Lockwood."

"But that name, Tina Dalbrige, or something similar. It rings a bell."

"Whether it does or doesn't, is immaterial," she said.

"You'd be allowing a killer to go free." Yeah—I was laying it on a bit thick, but subtleties were never my strong suit. I could bend the truth as well as the next guy, didn't matter I was in the righteous halls of our dear Lord and Savior, hallowed be thy name.

The Mother Superior fingered her gold cross strung about her neck, her lips moving, perhaps repeating a string of Hail Mary's for what she was about to do.

"You must make exceptions if there's a need," I said, giving her a necessary push.

"And you believe you have that need," she said.

"I knew Diana Gilbert close to twenty years ago. She was my teacher. The fact she returned to New Haven just recently, and was killed, tells me, she knew her killer. Either the child she gave up for adoption, or her husband."

"Or both," said the Mother Superior.

I hadn't thought of that. The two of them in cahoots.

"You have a devious mind," I told her.

"I've been accused of worse," she said. "Comes with the calling, I suppose." She attempted a smile and failed. "Whether by coincidence or design, four months ago we had a break-in. Nothing taken, but our files had been ransacked, flung about the office, a terrible mess to sort through and refile. You say she was your teacher, struck down and killed."

I informed her, it had been all over the news, hoping to shore up my argument.

The Mother Superior rang for one of the sisters, speaking quietly with the woman upon her arrival, whereby the second nun departed, returning some twenty minutes later with the information I was after. A name. Now all I needed was an address.

* * *

During my absence, Greta had been hard at work, catching up on the correspondence which included the requisite invoicing, licking stamps, addressing envelopes. She let her fingers do the walking through the local directory while I caught up on a couple of crossword puzzles.

Ten minutes later, she handed me a pink slip of paper. "They live on Mitchell Drive near East Rock Park not far from New Haven High."

Just peachy, the exact location where Bobbi and I attended classes.

"With luck, the son, or the adoptive parents will speak with me," I answered, grabbing my trusty fedora once again.

"Go get 'em, tiger," Greta chortled, which was exactly what I did.

I didn't bother phoning, why put the wind up? The parents, both well into their fifties were reluctant to speak with me at first. I had to use the ol' *I can go to the cops* routine, which eventually wedged open a crack, an opportunity to ask my questions.

"You adopted your son Godfrey on the 10th of November 1956," I told them.

Neither of them confirmed nor denied. "I spoke with the Mother Superior at the Catholic diocese in Jackson Heights. She gave me your names."

"She shouldn't have done that," sneered the husband, him in a wheelchair, something to do with heart troubles and high blood pressure. "We were told it would be kept confidential."

"A woman has been killed," I responded. "You may have read about it. Not far from here. Found near Mill River."

"We read about it," said the wife. "What's it to do with us?"

"I believe she was the birth mother of your son. If he knew of her existence, the cops will have questions."

"He didn't know," snapped the husband. "Freda and me, we were never told her name."

"But he knows he was adopted," I said.

The wife nodded. "We told him when he was twelve. He said it was no big deal. Lots of kids are adopted. As far as he's concerned, we're his parents, nothing further to discuss."

"Did Diana Sunderland ever visit you?" I asked. "Did she try to see her son?"

"No, why would she?" snarled the husband. "She's never been to the house, not to my knowledge."

"Nor mine," said the wife. "I think it's time you leave. We've nothing more to say."

"Where's your son now?" I asked.

"At school. He's in his final year at New Haven High. Track and field this time of day. He's a sprinter, and a good one. They run drills after class."

I plunked my fedora on my head, offered up a thank-you, and departed.

Time to visit New Haven High, my old stomping grounds. Neither Bobbi nor I had been on any sports team, our area of expertise much more cerebral such as reading glossy magazines and dime-store paperbacks, the racier the better, while smoking ourselves silly out behind the gymnasium.

A short time later, I met with the kid after getting a couple of chums to point him out. I told him what I was after. "Meet me back here in ten minutes," he said. "I'll take you to my locker." He then headed off to the change rooms. After that, he gave me what I needed. Proof to nail the son of a bitch.

* * *

A week later, Corrigan arrested Paul Sunderland for the murder of Diana Gilbert.

He stopped by just shy of quitting time, Greta having clocked out early. Corrigan looked worse for wear, lack of sleep no doubt working the case, his dark eyes brooding and thoughtful, his manner, however, elated. I knew the feeling.

I poured each of us a stiff bourbon while he unwrapped another piece of gum, rolled the silver and dropped it in the ashtray.

"Just as you suspected," he said. "Sunderland followed the wife from New York. He thought she was having an affair, the phone calls, letters written and received. When he saw her near the river with that kid, he figured it was a repeat performance of what she'd done years back, accused of sexual misconduct with that minor."

I interrupted. "I thought Sunderland didn't know about that."

"He knew but kept quiet. A lie by omission."

"It's been known to happen," I observed.

Corrigan leaned back in his chair, drank half of his drink in one go, set the glass on my desk. "The kid left, and that's when Sunderland lost it, bearing down on his wife with that rock he'd picked up, threatening her, thinking he'd scare her into a confession."

He then explained Diana wouldn't stop crying which meant, as far as Sunderland was concerned, the tears proved her guilt, caught in the act. He half wondered if the guy was breaking it off, or threatening to do so. Or maybe he'd threatened to go to the cops, or God forbid, what if it was blackmail, the reason for the tears. Sunderland didn't give Diana a chance to explain. He acted on impulse—judge, jury and executioner, smashing her skull with that rock, something any able-bodied American would do, according to Sunderland, if they too had learned their wife was committing a felony of the most despicable kind. How dare she!

"Once he started, blow after blow, he found he couldn't stop, no regrets, no remorse."

"Sounds like a real peach," I responded, Corrigan now in possession of the incriminating letters, what Godfrey Wheeler had given me at the school, letters he'd received from Diana and hidden in his locker, not wanting his parents to see them, to cast doubt on where his loyalties lie.

He'd agreed to meet with Diana, setting up that rendezvous near the river. He then let loose, no holds barred, simply telling her to get the blazes out of his life. He demanded she stop with the letters, and no more phone calls disrupting his classes. That left Diana in tears, her hopes dashed. At that exact moment, Sunderland entered the clearing. He saw Godfrey leave, jumping to his own conclusions about what his baby blues were giving him, and proceeded to end Diana's life.

"According to Sunderland," said Corrigan, "they'd drifted apart over the years, barely speaking. And now, his reputation was about to be shot down in flames. He'd worked hard to become a reputable attorney-at-law—university, law school, a year articling, investing in his future after he left the army, taking advantage of the GI bill. With what his eyes were giving him, his wife was about to destroy it all."

"So, what you're saying, Sunderland knew about the scandal but not about the kid."

Corrigan nodded. "His family, they were only too happy to fill him in on the sordid details when he got back from Korea. He'd have none of it, believing Diana was framed, the other teachers with their petty jealousies, especially the women. He's now saying, he should've listened, never married the gal."

"Marriage isn't for everyone," I echoed.

Again, Corrigan nodded. "Learning about the kid knocked the starch right out of him. It wasn't until we shared that bit of news, after his arrest, he saw the error of his ways."

"Doesn't sound like a sweet life," I said.

"Nothing sweet about any of it," Corrigan growled. "If they'd bloody well talked to each other, been forthcoming with the facts, none of this would've happened."

"We all have secrets," I said, thinking of Bobbi and Greta who definitely knew a boatload of mine, all safely tucked away, the only gals I trusted.

Corrigan finished his drink, plunked his fedora on his head and departed.

I lit up a smoke, tossed the match, and sat back, feet on my desk, blowing a couple of smoke rings toward the ceiling fan. I then swiveled in my chair and took a gander out the window, knowing I may never be a farmer with a million horses or an actor playing a part, but hey—I was content with my life, that of a private eye with an impeccable track record, thanks to Greta, she keeping me on the straight and narrow.

I wondered what Barry Manilow would've made of that, hardheaded Lockwood living the life, everything sweet in my world, a New England boy, competing with the best of them despite my humble beginnings, no flippin' academic degree messing with my sensibilities.

Rain as Cold as Ice

Inspired by *Mandy* from the album
Barry Manilow II (1974)

Linda Kay Hardie

I smelled petrichor. That fresh, almost-electrical scent of approaching rain that soon became the fresh feel of teensy raindrops blowing into my face as I strode through the crosswalk toward the number 15 bus stop and sat on the cold metal-bar bench, which was divided into five seats so homeless people couldn't sleep there.

You might not think of a bus station as being redolent with fresh rain fragrance. Long before my car died and went to junkyard heaven, I remember the Greyhound station, with me as a young adult wrinkling my nose at the foul stenches: urine, body odor, cigarette smoke. And, of course, vomit. Not so anymore. Or here, anyway. RTC hires people to regularly wash down the sidewalks with brooms and buckets of soapy water.

It's not all peaches and cream, though. The bus schedules and coverage of Reno are shitty, to put it mildly. And, as I sat on the bench, the chilly tickle of drizzle drops ran down the back of my neck, because who was the goddamned fucker who designed the roofs to have a space between the roof and the building so that rain and snow fell on the people below, sitting on these benches waiting for their buses?

But I turned up the collar of my raspberry raincoat, foiling the felonious drizzle tickle. Speaking of felonious, there was Jerry, looking like the end of a three-day bender that never ended. That wasn't his name; I called him that because he looked like the German soldiers in the WWII movies I liked to watch on Turner Classic on my TV. But a sound that wasn't Jerry screaming obscenities grabbed my attention.

Wait. Did I hear an old Barry Manilow song? The chuff of bus brakes and traffic noises all around dwindled for a moment, and I distinctly heard an old ballad. I hadn't thought of his music in decades. Wait. That couldn't be Barry himself, could it? Nah. Manilow played the piano, not guitar. And he certainly couldn't have fallen this far down to be playing for tips in a bus station in Reno, Nevada. Right?

Plus, I'm sure I read something about Manilow doing a residency in Las Vegas these days. However, despite what everyone from outside the state thinks, those of us in northern Nevada don't drive down to the southern part for dinner in Vegas, then zip home the same day. It's an eight-hour drive each way, longer if you pay attention to speed limits, and all of it through empty deserts. That's why I wasn't sure.

Whoever this musician was, he played guitar well. I followed the gently-strummed melody.

The young man waiting in the Stead stop around the corner from my number 15 stop appeared to be homeless. A large knapsack with a bedroll strapped to the top leaned against the bus bench where he sat. He'd found a place to sit with a roof actually over it, so he and his guitar were dry. His hair was long and scraggly and his beard showed about a week's growth. My 1970s self felt that he should have been playing John Denver or Michael Murphey. One of the more hippie-like singers instead, not the showman Manilow.

He was playing one of Manilow's ubiquitous ballads, this one from 1978, "Ready to Take a Chance Again." At that age (I was 20), I was very much into broken-hearted love songs, and no one did those better than Barry Manilow. The radio stations played the song forever, it seemed.

Typical Manilow schmaltz, as my then-husband used to sneer at me. I stayed with him longer than I should have. Still, breaking up is hard to do, to quote a slightly earlier Sedaka song. But hell, what did Neil know about it?

Silence jolted me out of my reverie. The stranger was glowering at me. I was surprised he'd even noticed me. I'm a post-menopausal woman, which means I'm totally invisible to men. Most of the time.

"I'm sorry," I said. "I didn't mean to disturb you. I'm a big fan and I haven't heard any of Manilow's music in years."

His face softened, but I could still sense a wariness.

"You play so well," I added.

He looked down at his right hand, touching the strings. He plucked a few, then looked up at me. "My wife liked this old stuff. This 'un seemed appropriate somehow."

He said "liked" with a soft "ah" sound instead of the hard "eye." I guessed Oklahoma, so he was far from home.

I looked around. "Where is your wife? Is she traveling with you?"

His body language flickered from wary to vigilant to cautious. What? Quicker than I could form a coherent thought, he smiled and began plucking the guitar's strings, altering Manilow's sweeping ballad into a hillbilly dance tune. He drawled Manilow's lyrics to this transformed tune and tapped his foot to fit the new rhythm.

I chuckled. He was changing the subject on me. Did he have something to hide? I could play this game, too.

He slammed his hand onto the front of the guitar. I jumped.

"She's gone." He shoved the guitar into the battered case next to his feet, clicked the latches, then slid it under the bench. He looked up at me. "Ah don't know where I've been. Without her, I'm lost anyway, so I took off. Hitched some, rode some buses. Walked a lot."

"I'm sorry. Are you okay?"

"Not really, ma'am; thanks for asking. Have a seat?"

The bench with its armrests was wide enough for us to sit without touching, especially since he had a small duffel to his right, easily marking off his territory. I sat next to the grimy bag.

"You live here in Reno, ma'am?" he asked.

"Yes."

"Family? Kids?"

"No. I grew up in a different time. Everything was more conservative then."

"I don't understand, ma'am."

"I never dated in high school. My parents were strict and set a lot of rules for me. They did ask me about boys sometimes, but mostly they cautioned me not to ruin my life. If you think Nevada is conservative now, it was much worse 40, 50 years ago. And it's not like I was even interested in boys."

I looked up from staring at my feet. The young man seemed to have a look of sympathy in his face.

"Were they worried you were a lesbian? That you would face discrimination back then?"

"No. That didn't even cross their minds. They were worried I would get pregnant, drop out of high school, and then I wouldn't be able to support them in their old age." I stopped for a moment, the old feelings threatening to overwhelm me. "No, I was so far in the closet I didn't even realize it myself."

"You never got married?"

"I actually did support my parents for many years. I wasn't interested in men at all. It never occurred to me that I might be gay. There was never any question that I could live like that. I'm not sure what my parents would have done if I'd realized who, what I was."

"What do you mean? Like, kick you out of the house?"

"No. More like that they would both die of heart attacks at the thought. Or that they would kill me."

"That's harsh, ma'am."

I shrugged. Truth is truth. "When society began to loosen up in the 80s, I started to feel out of place in a way I never had before. And I started to be drawn toward more progressive ideas. But it wasn't until marriage equality passed in 2015 that it dawned on me that I might be a lesbian."

"That's good," he said. "Isn't it?"

I shrugged.

"You ride the bus a lot?" he asked.

"Yes. I'm retired. When my car finally died, I couldn't afford to buy another one. I have lots of time. The bus is actually pretty interesting. I like to watch the people."

"Heading anywhere special now?"

"Just the senior center."

He looked away. And I realized I hadn't been paying attention to the people at the station.

I shivered and glanced around, suddenly aware that I was sitting with a man I didn't know anything about. The bus stop was moderately busy. I've never felt afraid at the station or on any of the buses, despite what everyone says. People who ride public transit tend to be older and poorer than the general population. Retired people. Working people. I've never felt threatened on the bus. That's just rich people prejudice. Still. Some poor people are desperate enough to mug an old woman for her pennies.

And sure, I see the ones who could use a working mental health system. They're talking to people no one else can see. There was one guy who muttered threats to an invisible companion, ordering that incorporeal person to "leave these passengers alone!" Even when he got off my stop, I wasn't concerned. He didn't seem to have any interest in me. Last I saw him, he was standing on a traffic island, shouting at his intangible opponent to shape up because he was an undercover FBI agent and would bust him. Cars rushed by on the busy street. The snow was three inches deep and coming down like a blizzard. I hope he was okay.

I turned back to this companion. Something seemed off-kilter, but I wasn't frightened. It was broad daylight in a public place. But maybe I should at least ask a question or two in this one-sided conversation.

"Do you have family or friends in Stead? Sometimes it helps to be around familiar people when you're troubled."

"What's Stead?"

I pointed to the sign that listed where this stop's bus would be going, which was a small bedroom community north of Reno where housing prices were a bit lower.

"No. I'm just passing through. I was walking to the Greyhound station down the block when I saw all these benches and stopped to rest." He shook his head, like he was trying to dislodge bad memories. "My family never understood me. Never liked me much either."

Welcome to the club, I didn't say out loud.

"Do you need some help?" I did say. "Our community has some decent social services. The number one bus goes to the welfare office, even though they don't call it that anymore. I'm sure they could point you in the right direction. Or take the Virginia Line Rapid to the downtown library. That's closer. The librarians are nice and are used to helping people with no place to go."

"No. I'm doing all right, ma'am. I just need time. Time and space." He scowled.

"Do you want to talk about your wife?"

His face softened, and he appeared to be considering it.

"Her name was Mandy. That's why she liked Manilow, because he had that song. The music app on her phone found it for her. She always did like that sentimental stuff."

"Were you together long?"

"All our lives," he said. "All her life for sure." He barked out a laugh.

What? He said she left him. No, he said she was "gone," in what I now saw was a very ambiguous statement. Did she die? A lot of men fall apart when their wives or girlfriends die. Any rejection or change that leads to grief or extreme sadness.

Men aren't used to dealing with emotions. They always count on the women in their relationships to do all the emotional labor for them. Like in the Manilow song this guy had played, where the narrator is a man living alone, all quiet and withdrawn, isolating himself from the world. He's been hurt by life, rejected by a woman who left him to carry the load of his feelings all by himself. And in the song, he ends up getting to the point where he's healing and starting to think about taking chances with life again. Finding another woman to take this emotional burden for him.

That's when I realized that something was rotten in Reno. Really. Something literally smelled bad. It wasn't body odor; it was more like spoiled meat. What I'd thought was a small duffel bag next to me was actually a fanny pack, as we called them back in my day. Now they're often worn across the chest and called crossbody bags instead.

This one was filthy. The navy blue nylon was crusted with rusty-looking stains. The man saw my glance, and he grabbed the bag and slung it across his left shoulder, away from me. An object inside the bag, about the size of my fist, bounced.

I blinked. What had we been talking about? Umm. His wife, who was "gone."

"Well, that's awful that she just up and left you like that," I said.

The young man stared at my face for a moment. He wouldn't read anything there. My husband and my parents taught me how to hide what I was thinking and feeling. Those were hard lessons, but I learned them well.

"Had you been married long? Were there signs?" I asked.

He finally broke the stare and glanced over my shoulder. From the angle, I figured he was checking out Fireside Market, the small store across Fourth Street from the bus station.

"Sorry. I don't mean to pry," I said. "Hey would you like to get a drink?"

"No money," he mumbled.

"I'll buy us a bottle. There's a little store," and I turned to point at the one he'd been eyeing. "What's your poison?"

"What!"

"Sorry. That's something we used to say back in the day. What do you like to drink? If you don't mind walking over there, I'll give you some cash. My knees aren't what they used to be."

"Bourbon." He stood up. His eyes were flinty.

I unzipped my fanny pack, which was buckled around my waist. I pulled out a $20 and a $10. "Here. This should get us a bottle at mini-mart prices." I held the bills out to him.

His grey eyes relaxed as he slowly took the money. "I'll be right back. You'll watch my stuff?"

"Sure. I'm not going anywhere. Knees, remember?"

"I hope you won't be insulted if I don't leave this, ma'am." He picked up the guitar case. "This is my baby."

I smiled and waved my hand in a "no worries" sort of say, shaking my head for emphasis. The small stained bag hanging from his shoulder went with him, but he left his knapsack. He trusted me with his luggage.

The young man returned with the bottle in a plastic bag and two soda cups filled with ice. Thoughtful. Or just practical. Midmorning on a quiet weekday, we were able to surreptitiously pour drinks without running afoul of Reno's law against public drinking and RTC's rules about it on their property.

"Looks like Co' Cola this way," he said with a smile, raising his cup.

I tapped mine against it. "To Mandy."

His eyes clouded briefly, but he nodded, then downed the bourbon like it was the Coke it appeared to be. I followed his lead, and he smiled and nodded. Poured us each another.

"We was high school sweethearts," he said, sipping on this one. "There never was anyone else for either of us. She attracted boys like shit attracts flies, but she didn't want them. Just me. I was a pitcher for the baseball team, hopin' for a scholarship to OK State in Stillwater."

"You weren't a musician? I would have thought...?"

"That was just for fun. Sports is what's important. In Oklahoma and in life."

I took another sip of my drink. Bourbon is not my favorite. My husband loved it, and he made me drink it in the evenings after we got married. He wanted me to seem like I was a willing partner. Later, after he was gone, I found that I prefer scotch. Much more sophisticated drink.

"What were Mandy's plans?"

"She would go to OK State with me. Mandy planned to major in accounting. She loved numbers, could make them dance." He looked down in his cup, then lifted it and took a sip. "She wanted to learn everything about them so she could get a job at a big firm and take them for all they're worth."

My swallow of bourbon went down wrong, and I coughed.

"Pardon?" I said.

"Mandy wanted to be rich. She knew she could do it this way. Embezzlement, she called it. Robin Hood stealing from the rich folk. I was so proud of her smarts. The yearbook called her 'most likely to succeed.' And we figgered she could manage my earnings when I got on with the Rangers or Astros."

"So what happened?"

"I got her pregnant in our senior year. The condom broke. So close, yet so far. We got married right away, of course. Can't raise a bastard. It was a beautiful wedding, even though we did it in the courthouse. She wanted us to write our own vows. In mine, I promised to keep her always by my side. In hers, she gave me her heart."

He stopped and looked away. In downtown Reno, there's no distance to look away to, all the distances being filled with casinos and parking garages. He poured himself another drink, smaller now that our ice was pretty much gone, and refreshed mine.

"She had to drop out of college because of morning sickness. She blamed me. I came home each day as soon as I could between classes and after practice. But it wasn't enough. I came home one day to find her in bed, blood everywhere."

"Did she try to kill herself?"

"No! She tried to kill our baby. She'd asked if I would help her travel to Kansas or New Mexico for an abortion. Of course I said no. So instead she found someone to help her do it herself. But they botched it, made a mess of it."

While he glanced away again, looking into the distance of the past, I slipped out the small bottle I always carried in my fanny pack and poured the contents into his almost-empty cup. My fanny pack was closed again, the bottle out of sight, by the time he looked down at his cup.

He offered me the last of the bourbon, but I told him to go ahead. He poured it into his cup and downed it. He tossed the cup onto the pavement at his feet, then took his guitar out of its case and began to strum Manilow's most famous ballad.

But he didn't sing the lyrics, so I asked him what happened next. "Did she die?"

"I don't know if she would have survived all that blood loss. But she killed our child! She broke my heart. After she *gave* me her heart."

He picked the notes of the song, humming along except to sing his late wife's name where it came up.

"I don't feel so good, ma'am." He shook his head and carefully put away his guitar.

"I could go get us another bottle." I stood up from the metal bench.

He looked up at me. "She gave me her heart. She *promised* it to me. What else could I do? She was pretty much dead already. Pretty much dead."

He hugged the bag with the grimy rust stains on it. Then his head drooped and he stared at the pavement. I quietly backed away from him, still holding my cup. I had to be somewhere else when the vomiting started.

He made quite a spectacle when the Stead bus pulled into its slot. I was over waiting in the number 15 area, out of sight, chatting with a young woman from the Yucatan in Mexico. I'd dumped my cup in a covered trash can. No one questioned later remembered him being with anyone. He was just a drifter who'd been playing some old songs and drinking bourbon, trying to get to Stead.

⋆ ⋆ ⋆

26

I don't know how much of the story I told the young man was true. Maybe I am so closeted I don't know I'm gay. Or maybe I'm the A in LGBTQIA+, the ace. That's what the young folks call someone who's asexual, right? The idea of voluntarily having sex makes me want to throw up, so I think I qualify.

All my life I've had to be responsible for other people. First it was my father, then my husband. And after he disappeared, I had to care for my parents. My father died of a heart attack or something, and it was just me and my mother. Nothing I did was ever good enough for her. I finally got free from her. I don't know how to not be in charge and look after people. The only one I don't know how to take care of is me.

But I try. Oleanders aren't as easy to find in northern Nevada as in the Las Vegas area. But I've found it's worth the searching. A distillation of the leaves has come in handy for me more than once. If you're ever on a cook-out in a southern desert anywhere, be sure not to use oleander sticks for roasting your hotdogs. Not a good idea.

I don't know how to stop now. I have to watch out for the evil men, the killers, rapists, the abusers. Men like my father, who abused and raped me throughout my childhood, then sold me off at age 14 to his friend, who was a pervert, too, as well as being 30 years my senior. My husband George, thank god, began to lose interest in me when I turned 21. It took me three more years to figure out how to get away from him. No one ever found the body.

Sometimes there are women who remind me of my mother. Mom knew. Mom knew who and what Dad and George were and she didn't care. Did. Not. Give. A. Flying. Fuck.

It's up to me to take care of them. The perverts and the ones who enabled them. It's my responsibility because no one else ever would.

"FUCK!" A shout interrupted my ruminations.

Poor Jerry's benders never ended. This was one of the days when a switch inside his head tripped over, a breaker in his brain failed, and he started screaming out his anger at the world in one, sad, sorry, overused four-letter word. Over and over, over and over. Even George Carlin would have been sad at the sound of this fucking fury.

Jerry slumped his way out of my line of sight, but I heard him yelling, "Give me money!" Then a pause. "Not enough! More!" God damn. He was mugging someone again. I carefully looked around for a security guard. The last thing I wanted was to make myself visible to Jerry, to catch his attention. No guards visible. The screaming had ceased. Problem solved, I hoped. I spotted his mugging victim, a 30ish woman in a business suit who looked shaken but otherwise okay. Jerry wasn't a great person, but he never really hurt anyone.

Just a typical day at Reno's Fourth Street bus station. The number 15 arrived. I climbed aboard and rolled away from it all. What did the senior center have for lunch today? As if it mattered. Maybe I'll ride the bus back downtown after lunch and see who's around.

I think I'm ready to take a chance again.

Radical Boys

Inspired by *Mandy* from the album
Barry Manilow II (1974)

Adam Gorgoni

When I ran into Mandy at Walmart that day—literally ran into her shopping cart cause that place is always a nuthouse—she was barreling around the corner of the seafood section and crashed right into me. The impact knocked her sunglasses off and I felt my breath catch at the sight of the dark, eggplant-purple bruise around her right eye. There was a fresh red cut in the skin near the socket which had only begun to scab.

"Shit, I'm sorry," she said, frantically grabbing for the big round glasses and slapping them back on to cover her eyes. I didn't miss her wincing as she twisted back around to stand up. I'd broken a couple ribs junior year so I recognized that reaction. "Oh…hey Danny, it's you," she said, as she twisted back around, forcing a smile. "How are ya?"

"I'm OK, Mandy, how you doing?"

"I'm hangin' in there."

"Yeah? How's Brick?"

"Oh, you know…he's Brick." She tried a half-hearted laugh.

Yeah, I did know.

* * *

Brick Williams and I were just grade school kids when we first met and even then he was the big man on campus so to speak. Lean and athletic, budding movie star good looks, class clown who got away with anything and everything. Always picked first when they were choosing up teams.

Not like me. I was a fat kid, and I was real self-conscious about it. I think maybe that's why I always liked books so much. I could disappear into them, pretend I was one of King Arthur's knights—not Lancelot…that would be Brick—or that I was Sam Gamgee on the quest to destroy the One ring with Frodo. Brick had a natural gravity about him and he kinda took me under his wing, made me part of his posse. That mattered a lot to a hesitant, heavy kid who had no idea where, or if, he would ever fit in. But Brick also had an edge. He gave me the nickname "Porky" and would use it sometimes to get a laugh from the other kids. At least no one teased me when I was lost in the stories.

Course a lot of that changed by high school. By then I'd grown into my frame—I was still heavy but now I was more of a tank. Coach Cross moved me and Brick up to varsity in the middle of freshman year. Brick was the QB (of course) and I played left tackle, assigned to protect his blind side. You know, like that movie (although if you ask me the book was way better.) See, those two positions—it's a different kind of relationship. There's an unspoken understanding, a pact almost. Yeah, the quarterback gets all the glory and the girls. But inside he knows that he's nothing without his left tackle. It creates a bond that's hard to describe if you haven't been there. A mutual respect and dependence. Neither person is going to get what they want if the other one doesn't come through. I didn't mind the anonymity. I kind of liked it actually. When Brick would holler at us in the huddle that we weren't giving him enough time I'd usually just take it out on the guy in front of me. Every so often, though, if he pissed me off enough, I'd let my guy through just to remind Mr. Wonderful where his bread was buttered. We made state junior and senior year, but we lost in the championship game both years.

Back then Brick was the leader and he was fun to be around. We were teenage knuckleheads, always on the lookout for stupid ways to entertain ourselves, which wasn't easy in the rural hills of Eastern Pennsylvania. We'd toss eggs into people's houses, or steal a golf cart and ride around the course at the local country club, hiding the flags in the woods. Probably the stupidest, which we called "Radical Boys," consisted of drinking beers in the evening, revving Brick's Camaro, turning off the headlights, and sailing through four-way crossroads at a hundred miles an hour, Guns'n'Roses blasting from the radio, and us howling like a pack of wild dogs. Seatbelts strictly forbidden, obviously.

* * *

"Your boys were really sweet the other day when they were over," Mandy said, as we stood there in the awkwardness. "Little Jake offered to help me with my grocery bags. Very polite."

Our boys were just about the same age, so they were all growing up together and were thick as thieves.

"They're good boys," I said.

Her lips pressed together inward and her face collapsed a little, almost as if she were about to cry right then and there. But then she bit down on her lower lip and kept it together. I knew it wasn't the first time Brick had crossed the line. He'd always been jealous and proprietary over her, especially whenever she gave other guys what he interpreted as too much attention, which to him was all the time. But from the condition her face was in now, things had taken a real turn for the worse.

* * *

When Mandy Milliken transferred into Stroudsberg High in 9th grade she wasn't yet the Homecoming Queen knockout she was to become. She had a soft, round face and blonde Pippi Longstocking braids, skinny-legged, and knock-kneed, like a faun. Nobody paid much attention, but I fell hard. What I saw were her clear, intelligent blue eyes that sparkled like running water when she smiled. And Mandy had this aura of innocence, even frailty, the uncertain new girl in a school full of kids who'd grown up together. I could relate to that. Of course I'd never had a girlfriend, and I had no idea how to go about getting one. So mostly I just tried to drift into Mandy's orbit as often as I could, hoping I'd somehow have an excuse to talk to her. We'd exchange a few shy glances and "hi's" but that was the extent of it at the beginning.

My luck changed sophomore year when Mandy was in both my History and my English classes. By then at least I knew enough to sit next to her every chance I got, and one day after class, as she was slinging her backpack over her shoulder in the hallway, a few notebooks tumbled out. I hopped down and scooped them up. "Oh shoot, thanks," she said. "I'm such a ditz. You're Danny, right?"

The ice was broken and we soon started spending a lot of time together. Mandy was kind of a book nerd too, so we'd study together in the library, or hang out during lunch and free periods, share headphones and turn each other on to bands we liked. I even taught her a little about football. It was all platonic of course, because I was still paralyzed with shyness and had no clue how to get from here to there. I didn't have the maturity at the time to see that she wasn't any farther along in her romantic experience than I was. I got a good bit of teasing from the guys, including Brick, who had already been going all the way with some of the older girls who were on the faster track. It took months for me to find the courage ask her out on a proper date.

Finally, at the end of the year I steeled my nerves and invited Mandy to the movies. We saw *Fatal Attraction* and I can still feel the electric sizzle that shot through my groin when she grabbed for me during the rabbit scene and her nipple rubbed against my arm. Later, outside her house, I was incredibly nervous, literally shaking, trying to get up the nerve to try to kiss her. And then she smiled softly and pulled my face down and the shaking stopped.

Mandy was due to leave later that week to spend the summer with relatives in Arizona. We went for a walk the day before she left, held hands, and kissed some more at the end. Still naive and flush with my big breakthrough I figured that in the fall we would pick up where we left off. But that's not what happened.

When Mandy returned, the baby fat on her face had melted away. Gone were the braids, brushed out into big cascading 80's waves, and where before she'd been rail thin, she now had curves. And boobs. It was like Bambi had gone away for the summer and come back as Kim

Basinger. Everyone noticed. The boys were enthralled, and the clique of popular girls, who'd never given her a thought, closed ranks and started buzzing around her, hoping some of her newfound sex appeal would rub off.

And of course there was Brick, who registered Mandy's metamorphosis right away and zeroed in. She resisted his advances for a while. Looking back, I realize maybe she was waiting to see if I would fight for her. But I was too insecure to give up the safe, defined place in the confusing high-school pecking order that my friendship with Brick afforded me. I didn't fight. I didn't do anything. And eventually, she succumbed to the handsome quarterback who was hot shit and all.

After high school Brick went to Penn State, blew out his knee, and came strutting back to East Stroudsberg acting like he was some kind of injured war hero, swearing up and down that he was gonna rehab and go back. Instead, he let his parents set him up as manager at their Ace franchise. As we moved through our twenties and his glory days receded into the past, he got a little softer around the belly and a lot less charismatic. It was sad to watch him clinging to a version of himself that everyone else could see was long gone.

Not that I was doing any better. I worked my way through school as an auto mechanic and then I met Jessie. We stayed married long enough to have our boys, but it was never an easy relationship. I tried my best, but the truth is my heart was spoken for and I think Jessie knew it the whole time. Before the divorce, we'd double-date with Brick and Mandy sometimes. I'd catch Mandy staring at me across the table and find myself wishing I could rewind the years, rewrite the whole story, but there was nothing I could do. Now she was two kids in and trapped. And I couldn't help feeling it was at least partially my fault.

* * *

Mandy and I stood there in Walmart for another second, as the shopping cart superhighway rolled on by. She hadn't lost any of her unstudied beauty but she seemed smaller somehow. I could tell she was looking at me but her expression was hidden behind her sunglasses.

There were so many things I wanted to say. How much longer are you going to stand for this? Don't you know you can leave him? I never stopped loving you. But standing there in the Walmart seafood aisle, it was neither the time nor the place.

"Alright, well, it's good to see you," I finally said. Then we exchanged an uncomfortable, delicate hug. I wasn't sure but it seemed like she hung on a little too long before we separated and said goodbye.

* * *

That night I had dinner with my older sister Cathy. She was three years ahead of us in high school.

"I ran into Mandy today," I said.

"Yeah, how's she doing?"

"Brick hit her again. Really bad this time."

Cathy just rolled her eyes. She didn't have much patience for such things.

"At this point it's her own fault. I'd've been gone the second he touched me the first time."

"I know, but she's in a tough spot with the kids and all. Not everyone's as strong as you."

"She's going to be in an even tougher spot if he kills her." Cathy *is* strong, the strongest person I know. She sees things in black and white, calls it like she sees it, and doesn't take shit from anybody. Mom was sick a lot when we were growing up and Cathy was definitely the quarterback in our house.

"Anyway," she continued, "it's not really your business. She needs to handle it herself. If you try to get involved, you'll only make it worse."

That night I slept poorly, and the next day I couldn't concentrate in any of my early classes. By mid-morning I gave up and had my eighth graders read a Nick Adams story out loud and then break up into small groups to discuss. Next period I threw a pop quiz on Gatsby at my eleventh graders. I kept thinking about what Cathy said. I knew she was right. Mandy was in real trouble, that was for sure. I decided to reach out to Ed Ramchek.

* * *

Ed was a year ahead of us in school and played guard on the side opposite me. He was a quiet guy off the field and solid in games, always in the right place, executing his assignment. After high-school he did two tours in the Marines and fought in Iraq during Desert Storm. When he got back he went to the police academy and joined the Monroe County Sheriff's Department. Everyone liked Ed. He was one of us, stayed put in the community, contributed, started raising his family right here where we grew up.

After last class, before I was due to teach driver's ed, I ducked into the teacher's lounge and called the station.

"Hey, Bev, it's Danny Brunson."

"Hey, Danny, how you doing?"

"Just fine, Bev, thank you for asking. I'm looking for Ed."

"He's out on patrol, but I can call him for you."

"That'd be great. I'd love to talk to him in person if I can."

"Sure, baby, can you hold on?" After a minute or so she came back on. "Eddie says he can meet you at five-thirty on Elizabeth Street right outside school. Will that work?"

Ed rolled up right on time.

"Hey, Bruns. How's it goin'?"

"I'm good, Eddie, I'm good. How's Audrey and the kids?"

"Good. You know. Running us ragged as usual. So what's up?"

"It's about Brick and Mandy."

He sighed heavily.

"I guess I just…I ran into her yesterday and…I think he hit her again, bad this time. And I'm wondering if there's anything law enforcement can do about it."

"Shit Danny, I went up there once before. There's not much we can do if we don't catch someone in the act or the victim doesn't press charges. I can't arrest him just because she has bruises."

"Even if you know he did it?"

"Not when she swears he didn't touch her, no."

"Well, she was really hurt this time and I just…could you just go and talk to her again. For me. See what she says now. It's getting out of hand."

The radio in his car crackled.

"Does Brick know you know?"

"No."

He spat into the gutter. "Aw hell, Danny, yeah of course I'll go talk to her."

"Thanks Eddie. You're the man."

* * *

I was home having dinner alone watching Jeopardy when the phone rang a few hours later.

"Hey Bruns, it's Ed."

"Hey, Ed."

"Well you're right, she's pretty beat up. She swears she slammed her head into the corner of a cabinet and that's why. I told her she didn't have to be afraid to tell me the truth and she started crying but she wouldn't budge on her story. I told her we couldn't protect her and these things usually don't end well. I'm not sure what else I can do, unless she changes her mind. I tried."

"Alright thanks Eddie. I appreciate it."

"See you at the game Friday?"

"Yep. I'll be there," I said, but I felt like a pile of shit when I said it.

* * *

I rolled around in bed that night. Very little sleep. Hollow and frustrated, a shadow of myself. Mandy's situation was unsustainable. Someone had to do something, before the worst happened. At the same time, as disgusted as I was with Brick, I still felt connected to him. We'd been forged in the same fire, shared experiences that bound us together. I wanted to believe that the old Brick was still in there somewhere. Self-centered, entitled, but not a complete asshole. Not a batterer. And if I could get through to him, get him back on track, maybe I could save him from himself and save Mandy in the process. That doesn't make much sense when I hear myself say it now, but that's how I felt.

* * *

That Friday Stroudsberg High had a big game against Northampton. Maybe high school football in Eastern Pennsylvania isn't quite the Friday Night Lights of West Texas, but don't try to tell that to anyone who lives here. The games are huge events in the community and everyone shows up, students, teachers, parents, alumni, and pretty much everybody else. There's food and flasks and flags and bands and announcers and cheerleaders. A real happening. Ex-players, especially the good ones, are kinda celebrities. So I knew Brick would be there, as would Mandy and their kids. It wasn't my weekend with my boys, so I'd be going solo.

I milled around for a while, greeting folks, patting backs, making small talk. But really I was scouring the scene, waiting. Finally, they arrived. Mandy had on enough makeup to hide her bruises.

I made my way over and we all exchanged hugs, which felt weird.

"Hey Professor," Brick said, his latest sobriquet for me. "How's it hangin'?"

"Little to the left," I said, falling into our familiar juvenile banter, and regretting it immediately.

"You ready? Let's go sit."

Brick's family had a row of season tickets where we always sat.

"Hi, Mr. Williams," I said, shaking his dad's hand. "Nice to see you."

"You too Danny, as always."

* * *

At halftime, most of the spectators had moved over to the concession area and Brick took his boys out on the field to throw the ball around which was his usual MO. Mandy and I found ourselves standing alone on the sidelines watching them. No sunglasses this time. Tears were forming in her eyes and she brushed them away.

"I can't do this anymore. I'm so scared."

"You don't have to stay with him."

"I know. I made a decision last night, and I tried to tell him I was leaving but he went crazy and started yelling and throwing things. He said he'll never let me leave. He'll kill me first." Then she looked up at me and it was like we were transported back fifteen years, standing there outside her front door, the future yet to be written. "What happened to us Danny? Why did you let me go?"

It wouldn't have hurt worse if she'd physically stabbed me in the heart. But there was a goodness in the pain. A validation.

"I'm so sorry, Mandy. I'd do anything to go back again and get another chance."

"Yeah, me too," she said, almost in a whisper, her words hanging there, vibrating in the night air.

* * *

I spent the second half in a strange altered state. The sounds and details of the game were a washy blur. All my senses were hyper-focused on Brick. He spewed a constant stream of nasty, childish insults at the kids on the visiting team. He led his boys in a chant of *Hey ref, you suck.* At one point he jumped up to complain about a penalty call and spilled half his beer on Mandy, who was sitting next to him. "Watch it, babe," he said, glancing briefly in her direction before turning right back around. And when he said it, I felt something go cold inside and click into place. It was like a veil had been lifted and I was seeing all three of us clearly for the first time, myself most of all. There should be an eighth deadly sin: complicity. And sometimes there's just no middle ground.

* * *

The game was close. With under a minute left, our Mountaineers were heading in for the go ahead score when somebody missed a block and we gave up a sack fumble and lost by two.

"Well, that sucked," Brick said, as we stood up and started to file out. "How could the protection break down in the crucial moment like that. It's inexcusable."

"Gotta come through when it counts," I said. "Hey, wanna go over to Diamond's for a couple? Been a little while."

"Sure, buddy, that sounds great."

"I'll drive."

"No problemo." He turned to Mandy. "Babe, you take the boys home, OK?"

* * *

Diamond Jim's was our usual hangout and we settled into a booth and ordered a couple of beers.

"You hungry? I'm hungry," said Brick.

He ordered the ribeye (he always ordered the ribeye) and I ordered the salmon. We toasted to the Mountaineers and Brick leaned back against the wall, feet up on the seat, like he owned the place.

"So how's it going, Bruns? You keeping busy? Schooling up the young ones?"

"Always," I said.

"I've been reading *The Runaway Jury*. The new John Grisham? It's really good." For some reason Brick always wanted to let me know what he was reading, or maybe just that he *was* reading.

"Yeah, I heard that," I said. "I'll put it in the pile on my nightstand."

Eventually, the waitress brought our food and we tucked in. Small talk over dinner. The game. The kids, as if there was nothing amiss. I had a plan, but I felt like I owed him one last chance.

"Brick, I saw Mandy the other day, at Walmart."

He flinched a little but said, "Oh yeah? She didn't mention it."

"Yeah, we actually bumped shopping carts and her glasses fell off." He leaned back and took a swig, but he didn't say anything. I pushed. "You want to talk about it?"

His eyes closed and he blew out a big breath. I knew we were at some kind of a breaking point and I could barely breathe. Finally, he opened his eyes and turned to me.

"You know I love you, Bruns. We've been through the wars together and you've always had my back. But this is between me and my wife, and it's a boundary you need to respect."

"OK, but you can't keep…"

The bottom of his glass made a violent, fire-cracker sound when he banged it back down on the table, loud, but hollow, like a rifle shot somewhere way off in the woods when you're hunting. His voice rose in pitch, tight and unhinged. "Look, mind your own fucking business, OK? When I need your help, I'll ask you for it!"

So there it was.

"OK, Brick," I said. "Sorry, but I had to mention it."

We talked for a while more and I steered the conversation back to more familiar territory. The Eagles crappy season. Monica Lewinsky and Bill Clinton. Things I knew would put him at his ease. And sure enough he went back to his more casual, the world is my oyster, demeanor. I played along, and soon it was like nothing had happened.

"I gotta take a leak," I said. "Order us one more round."

"You got it."

To get to the bathrooms at Diamond Jim's you walk past the hostess station in front, but when I got there, I turned left and went out to the parking lot. I drive a Ford Ranger and it's got a feature that allows you to disable the passenger side airbag. It's there because if you're driving young kids around, the airbag can be more dangerous for them if there's a crash. It's pretty simple to use. There's a switch on the passenger side of the console and you just put in the ignition key and turn the switch to off.

When we were near the end of our beers, I caught his eye.

"Hey, Brick. How about a little Radical Boys on the way home? For old time's sake."

He grinned. "Sounds like a fantastic idea, professor."

* * *

"Let's have some tunes," he said as we got in the car, turning on the radio. "Oh, shit, this is that new group. The Wallflowers? The guy is Bob Dylan's son."

We pulled out, spitting gravel into the road, the "One Headlight" bass pumping the air all around us.

"Remember. No seatbelts," he said. "Radical boys."

"Not on your life," I said.

We both knew the roads by heart and there were a number of four-way crossroads, but I had a specific one in mind.

"Let's do the one on 447, toward Analomink," I said.

"It's your world, boss."

There was a tight curve a hundred yards or so before this particular spot so I'd have to slow down to negotiate that before I could get back up to speed. But I had no intention of reaching the crossroads going anywhere close to a hundred. At that kind of speed, no seatbelt or airbag is going to save you. If you're going forty, though, and you're wearing your seatbelt, and your airbags deploy properly, your chances of escaping without serious injury aren't bad. I learned that getting my driver instruction certification. Without the safety mechanisms, even at forty your odds are slim.

"Turn it up," I said just as we headed into the turn, and while his attention was on the radio I reached up with my left hand and pulled the seatbelt strap down across my chest, quietly snapping the buckle into place. I started to accelerate out of the turn, and flipped off the headlights. Brick tilted his head back and started yipping like a Confederate soldier on the attack, lost in a world that no longer applied to me. We were going about thirty-nine when I yanked the wheel to the right, toward the trees on the passenger side and braced myself for impact.

* * *

Mandy and I still haven't spoken about exactly what took place that night. Not with words anyway. But there have been moments, in the ensuing years—when I'll catch her staring at me across the table during dinner, kinda like she used to, blue eyes moist with what I believe is gratitude and understanding, although there's always a trace of sadness also. I think she knows I protected her in the only way I could think of that would give us both another chance. All four of the boys are on varsity now. Jake is an O-lineman like his dad. He has a real shot at college ball, but we'll see.

I Write the Songs

Inspired by *I Write the Songs* from the album
Tryin' to Get the Feeling (1975)

Maya St. Clair

ET IN PALOMA EGO
(Nadia Kaur, *The Economist*)

'It's a shame,' says my guide, who goes by Tover, as he leads me into thigh-high water, deeper through the cavelike bowels of what once was the Paloma nightclub. His torch casts a bobbing spotlight on the wreckage: dripping beams, a ruined grand staircase, tables at haphazard angles rising from the water. Overhead, colonnades in the shape of palm trees crest towards the ceiling; below, more plastic trees form jungle-like enclosures by the booths. I slosh after my companion and disrupt large, floating mats of grime and fungus.

Through this midnight swamp, half-artificial and half-real, Tover's voice is echoing. 'Nice place, my nan said. Everybody came here. She didn't believe all that about Lane Britton and the rest.'

'Do you?' I ask, as he extends a hand to help me up an intact region of the stairs.

He shrugs. 'Dunno. There's always so much going on. Like, in a place, you know.'

Tover, who won't tell me his real name, is one of the many local urban explorers who have braved the ruin of the Paloma since its closure in 1985. He's been here many times, and he supplied me with the fishing waders I wear now. When we reach the balcony, he crouches and nods studiously: at the plastic canopy below, the plexiglass toucans hanging upside-down. He gestures to my camera. 'Best view's up here. Should get some pictures while we can.'

* * *

DEMOLITION ON HORIZON
FOR NOTORIOUS NIGHTCLUB
(*The Guardian*)

BRIGHTON—At its heyday, the Paloma nightclub and hotel was a haunt for some of rock and disco's most iconic figures. A palatial—some say chintzy—Mecca for tourists and locals alike, it hosted shows and late-night revels for the likes of Ted Royce, Chadwick Howard, and Lane Britton. After a series of highly-publicized deaths and financial difficulties in the 1980s, the Paloma shuttered and fell into disrepair; now, news of the ruin's impending demolition has provoked mixed reactions throughout the community, especially those who experienced its excesses firsthand.

'Oh, it was lovely,' says Mona Robins, 87, with a sigh. 'Those pink walls and the dancers. I wish they could have saved it, fixed it up. You know, Ted Royce once kissed me there. Leaned me down and just kissed me. He was radiant. It's such a shame.'

'No, no,' says Marcy Nesbitt, 86. 'I always got an awful feeling in that place. Like being watched. I only went so often because *you* did.'

The Paloma's legacy is one of both worldly glamor and artistic inspiration: musicians and bohemians flocked there and performed on its four stages. Many stayed in formal (sometimes informal) residencies, inspired by its dazzling, exaggerated atmosphere. Ted Royce performed a string of intimate concerts in its Midas Room, and hits like Lane Britton's 'Sweet Teeth' and 'Belle Dame,' and Chadwick Howard's 'Love Is Strange Indeed,' had their origins in the Paloma. But the revels had a darker side: drugs flowed freely, and many of the nightclub's most devoted occupants met their ends within its walls. Rumors of curses, killers, and pacts with malign spirits circulated wildly before its closure.

* * *

REMEMBERING THE PALOMA
(*The Stage*)

[...] Lewis Dinn, 75, is a retired music correspondent and past frequenter of the club, currently at work on a comprehensive history of the Paloma (*Paloma: Bright Lights, Vice, and Music at Brighton's Infamous Nightclub,* out next year at Bloomsbury). A thin figure in a lavender suit, Dinn carefully stubs his cigarette and flips through the archival documents he has laid out for us.

'It was called the Rose, initially,' he says, holding up a sepia-toned photograph of an old marquee from 1928, and another of a long-haired woman with kohled eyes. Dinn tells us that in 1930, the club was named for her: Paloma Gallo, singer and mistress of founder John Allgyer. A probable immigrant of obscure origins, Gallo left Allgyer in 1930, and does not seem to have returned, despite the gesture. ('Perhaps,' Dinn remarks drily, 'she knew what mishaps were to follow.')

More photographs take us through frozen moments of the club's long, varied history: the Palm Room in 1945, where a group of Black American G.I.s pose with burlesque dancers; trumpeter Joe Carmen laughing as a parrot is placed on his shoulder, 1947; the funeral procession of Allgyer, who died in 1951 during a celebration of the club's twenty-third anniversary. According to news articles, a stage-lift rope gave way beneath him, sending Allgyer falling headfirst into the stage.

As Dinn replaces the documents in plastic sleeves, we ask him: *is there a curse?*

He seems fatigued by the question, or at least the scientific yes/no nature of it. 'As a writer, I have oft "believed" the curse for pure aesthetic reasons. Otherwise, I am not qualified to say. Perhaps there was some grand, malefic "Curse." Perhaps there was only the lower-case, endemic "curses" of the time: excess and exploitation, drugs of immediate availability and nearly endless quantity. I will say this: I was a young man once—a young gay man. And the Paloma, even for its flaws, was an environment in which my eccentricities and foibles were welcomed. I had quite a few adventures there, many of which I cannot print, and I maintain that for better or worse its story must be told.'

Dinn posts his research on the blog *Paloma Archives,* and in 2014 published a memoir of his correspondent days, *20th Century Boy: Adventures in the 70s Music Scene* [...]

* * *

ET IN PALOMA
(Kaur, ctd)

In the Jurassic twilight, Tover and I sit down for our sandwich lunch, hunkering on an old mirrored table like castaways on a remote island. He points out pale, sickly-looking frogs as they bounce by.

We're in the Midas Room, one of the Paloma's smallest lounges. Booths, covered in a thick black roughness that Tover speculates was orange shag, form little coves along the border of the room. I shine the torch into the water and can just barely discern a grid below, covered in silt. I recognize it from some pictures I'd seen online: a light-up stage/dancefloor, where Ted Royce gave intimate after-midnight concerts in the 70s.

As we finish our lunch, a bigger groan echoes within the building, one that lasts for several seconds. Deep, wet-sounding, intestinal. Tover, looking up, stops chewing for a second.

'Is that typical?' I ask.

'Kind of,' he says. He explains that many old Brighton sites, built so close to the sea, have weird foundations. We should probably be quick, he says, and finish our tour through the building. I munch faster, and wipe breadcrumbs from my hands into the water. A shoal of plastic cocktail swords floats by.

* * *

PALOMA SHUTS DOWN TWO WEEKS
AFTER DEATH OF TED ROYCE
(*The Brighton Argus,* April 5, 1979)

[...] According to eyewitnesses, the singer, who had struggled through the last few numbers of his set, collapsed onstage. He was transported to his rooms to await medical attention and was pronounced dead by paramedics at 4:12 a.m. yesterday. A cause has not yet been announced.

Local residents expressed their shock and rage at the Paloma, with some blaming management. 'It's an unpleasant place, probably full of mold, or asbestos,' says Marcy Nesbitt, 40. She had attended some previous shows by Royce, and described the Midas Room as 'damp, disgusting,' and the singer's bearing as 'unsettled.'

Mona Thompson, 41, teared up when asked about the singer's death. 'I've never met a kinder man. He even kissed my hand. Such beautiful music. It always was.'

An anonymous source reports that Royce, long interested in 'new age' spirituality, had in the weeks before his death consulted psychic and dianetic experts about the nightclub and the Midas Room specifically.

* * *

A BIT ON TED ROYCE
(posted on Paloma Archives)

I wrote this piece in '79 for *New Musical Express,* not long after his death. *NME* prudently decided not to publish it; its mood and imagery were largely inappropriate for times of mourning. Enjoy (or don't); I stand by it as a portrait of his final days. xxxx -LD

The Midas Room, his manager told me, was all about control. Four walls. Four-sided stages. He had become obsessed with numerology (a source close to his manager told me), and believed the number would fend off a presence that appeared to him in dreams. Four elements, four cardinal directions, four performance rooms at the Paloma. He had recently wed his sloe-eyed fourth wife, and permitted no other women to touch him.

Perhaps there was something to this numerology. During the shows, an immanence hung in the room, a sense of concentrated energies and sacred expiation: dim gold shadows, spotlight-heat, the floor whose crucial corner squares must remain lit-up at all times. In those last days, he had become—and hence the eerie, mighty quality of those performances—a cosmic actor, John Dee in a coruscating suit, tracing unseen lines across the stage, holding some obscure fabric of the world together. His sweat was blinding; his voice low and resonant. His blood (I'm told) was found to be an ichor of amphetamines and painkillers that would have long since killed a normal man. He broke apart like an atomic particle in an immense state of activity, unable to sustain his own tremendous energies.

I asked my sources: why did Royce choose to remain there, in a state of interdimensional siege? If—as is widely believed—the place itself was deeply evil? Answers to these questions were less certain, but I gleaned a sense that for Ted Royce, to extricate himself from the Paloma would have been impossible. *He had communed with, hotwired himself to some genius loci that fueled and inspired him, even as it drained and tormented. On some deep level, Royce knew that the fight would kill him—as eventually it did.*

* * *

TRANSCRIPT OF SHOW FROM VIDEOTAPE
(April 4, 1979)

THE MIDAS ROOM

TED ROYCE: This is a song [...] wanted to do for you all [...] You remember that song, Tip?

TIP LEMARE (GUITARIST): [...]

TED ROYCE: Just feel it. Okay. Okay.

    [song begins]

> Can't see nothin'
> Can't see nothin' when you're gone
> Can't hear nothin'
> Can't hear nothin' when you're gone
> Can't see nothin' or hear nothin'
> And I don't what I've done
> [...]

* * *

PALOMA DIRECTOR EXITS
(*The Brighton Argus,* November 1975)

Citing personal reasons and desire to explore different business ventures, Calvin Pearce, owner of the Paloma nightclub, has announced his exit as primary shareholder and director of the business. Pearce's tenure was marked by diminishing profits for the Paloma, as well as the tragic death of controversial rock icon Lane Britton last year. Public complaints about safety proliferated.

Replacing Pearce is London entertainment mogul James R. Gill, who expressed his eagerness to get the nightclub 'back on track' with higher-profile residencies and construction of an intimate performance space and dance room.

* * *

ET IN PALOMA
(Kaur, ctd)

In the Royal Room, one of the booths has been cleaned by the urbex group, its mirrored backsplash wiped and glistening. Tarot cards, lace panties, and a single silk scarf form a shrine. Tover dredges through his backpack and withdraws a miniature vodka bottle. 'This was Britton's booth, if you couldn't tell,' he says. 'I'm not really a fan, but Nan was.' He hands me a second bottle, and I add it to the votive pile. 'Is the scarf appropriate?' I ask.

Tover shrugs. The water here is low enough that I can slip into the booth and (since it's been cleaned) sit down on the cracked vinyl, staring out at the room and its smeared mirrors.

* * *

20th CENTURY BOY
(Lewis Dinn, p. 183)

He was always in the center of the booth. Arms out, often around someone. But the eyes always fixed outward, keen and dark under the lashes. 'Lane Britton is a sphynx,' I'd written once, an assessment that I later heard he had enjoyed. As his eyes followed mine through the candescent smoke, I fumbled and grew flushed: I suspect he had such an effect on anyone with working glands and the ability to understand the beautiful.

I did not notice, then, how sunken those eyes were beneath the sparkling red paint and the reflected cigarettes. Or how his nails had been chewed, or how the gums were blanched. I drank something to shore up my courage, and approached. A ringed hand waved me closer. He spoke murmurously, always with a trace of smile on his lips. Wasn't I that nice boy from NME, who had been so fair to his last album? I ended up beside him (as I reported at the time), and then under his arm (as I did not).

Somebody slid a little mirrored tray my way; he watched me bend down over it, himself not partaking. I had gotten one point wrong, he said, in that review of mine. I'd written that Lane Britton was rock's future. This was silly. Rock had no future. Rock was nothing but a constantly-recurring past. His lips were at my shoulder, leaving trails of metallic glitter. He was working on another record. Would I like the exclusive?

* * *

REVIEW: *RED SPACE*
(Aug 1973, *Rock! Magazine*)

[...] To his credit, Britton has at least brought earthiness to 'glam,' and always owed more to Jim Morrison's violent, disturbed heroic figures than the ethereal, go-boogie Supermen one finds in Bowie or T. Rex. On *Red Space,* Britton's fascinating grimness *almost* justifies the overwrought pretension of it all. Don't believe the rapture in *NME;* Britton's lyricism seldom rises to the levels of his early stuff, and when it does (mostly on 'Sweet Teeth'), it's undercut by preening Eastern trappings (sitar! sistrum!) and layers of drone-pedal guitar.

* * *

20th CENTURY BOY
(Dinn, ctd)

As we drifted further from the frenzy of the main hall, my steps began to slow. By then, our party was myself, Britton, and a few groupies; I noticed in the hallway light that they were younger than I'd thought. Two brunettes, weirdly similar.

He teased me when I paused outside his room. Maybe, he suggested, this was all too much for me. Maybe I'd prefer to interview those Eurovision groups performing at the Bowl next door. I shook my head. He led me in, a filamentary hand about my waist.

As I watched, he stretched out on the floor. His pale limbs gave off a faint luminescence in the shadows. This was how he'd written 'Sweet Teeth,' he explained, and many other songs that Atlantic had not allowed him to release: by lying in pitch-darkness, supine, waiting for lappings of influence against his mind. As a kind of demonstration, he drew me downward and posed me like himself, arms at my sides. He explained that the Tibetan monks did this, shutting themselves in coffins for days at a time. The end-goal was to be receptive. To what? I asked. He laughed. To nothing, he said. Shadow pressing on the eyes. He offered to enhance my liminal experience with a silk scarf. I declined.

Britton put on some demos of the unreleased songs. They were very good, and he hoped Atlantic would relent about the one called 'Belle Dame.' To accommodate me, he flicked on a lamp (draped with a piano shawl) and told me about some Persian empress who'd buried noblemen alive as sacrificial offerings. I remember the details of the room exactly: stained wood panels, a brass ashtray, heaps of velvet shirts. His eyes in their red coronas, and the rhinestones on his skin.

* * *

CORONER'S REPORT
(September 6, 1974)

The deceased was found in his personal hotel suite, alone, in a clear state of death. Paramedics were called; resuscitation not attempted. Around the throat of the deceased was a scarf, tied tightly around the neck, with the deceased's hands on the object.

Toxicological analysis, as determined from a blood sample, revealed the presence of alcohol at a level of .02%, indicating prior consumption but no impairment. Cocaine was detected at levels of .01 mg/L, indicating minor contact exposure rather than direct consumption.

Ligature marks were found where the scarf had been tied. Multiple abrasions were observed on the neck, consistent with the subject's own tissue found under the fingernails. It is likely that the deceased, in a high state of stress, attempted to remove the scarf but was unable. Neck vessels and jugular vein were compressed, indicating a sudden and unintentional loss of consciousness. I find that the deceased, Sebastian Lane Britton, perished accidentally, by asphyxiation of a self-inflicted nature.

* * *

'BELLE DAME' (1974)
[…] You don't understand
What is to be proud
To be proud is to give
To give in and give out
She prepares the places
Where I am allowed
She is the image
And I am the shroud

* * *

ET IN PALOMA
(Kaur, ctd)

The structure groans again. Tover looks more distressed this time. Before we can confer, a crawling lurch moves the ground under us. Not an earthquake or vibration: more like the tread of a tank, rolling, shifting us on top of it. I let out an involuntary yelp when I see the water—the whole plane of water that has spanned the room—begin to tilt.

Tover makes us stay put for a few seconds, then ushers me out of the booth. We make our way to higher ground. He stands in front of me, parting the slight current. Pieces of debris thump against him, then slide past.

(I've since asked him if he regrets this decision, to go first. He says he doesn't and gives me a forced shrug. He says: he had to make sure I was safe; he would have done it, even if it meant much worse for him; it's not like he was hurt; etc. The color drains out of his cheeks, and he pulls his hands backwards as though from some invisible contagion.)

* * *

HOWARD DEATH RULED ACCIDENTAL
(*The Brighton Herald*, June 1968)

[...] Following public speculation, authorities have announced that Chadwick Howard, well-known singer who stayed at the Paloma during a string of U.K. shows, died accidentally of a handgun misfiring. An unnamed dancer, with whom Howard often shared a suite, was unavailable for comment.

Howard, who had famously stayed at the nightclub whilst writing his hit song, 'Love Is Strange Indeed,' had returned in hopes of rekindling this inspiration. According to rumors, his recent efforts at the nightclub had produced varying, often unfinished works. P. E. Carlisle, Howard's manager, told the *Herald* that 'out of respect for Chadwick Howard and his family, [the Paloma songs] will never be released.'

* * *

ON HISTORIOGRAPHY/THE LIST
(posted on *Paloma Archives*)

I am not too curmudgeonly to ignore my readers' most frequent request: a comprehensive list of singers, musicians, and artistic persons who have perished within the Paloma. I direct them to the source below, if they wish to indulge the base impulse to *collect* and *quantify*. It includes Royce, Britton, Howard, and the less-famous deaths from the Paloma's early history: Joe Carmen, 'Owl' Duplay, Frank Flynn, and of course John Allgyer.

I dislike such lists, and find them reductive. What was once a complex situational reality becomes compressed into disposable and superficial trivia; the experiential element translated into vulgar factoids for those who seek to impress and cite, not understand.

* * *

ET IN PALOMA
(Kaur, ctd)

We exit the same way that we came in. Several of the walls have broken along fault lines. Water gutters into the Palm Room; we can identify the currents from the different-colored dust and algae that flow into the shadows. Some of the plastic palms sigh as they fall.

For the first time, I feel like I truly understand the scale of the place. Rumbling issues from what sounds like miles away. The sulfurous white light of the torch flies up and down, a small firefly inside a black jar.

Once out of the Palm Room, we reach the stairway that will take us towards the exit. As I hold the torch, Tover takes a few exploratory steps, and gives me the nod. I'm about to join him when his foot falls through the wood. A black opening yawns underneath. He clutches at the railing and scrabbles for footholds, as water sloshes into the chasm. Something rises in the gap, and he begins to scream.

* * *

Dear Mr. Dinn,

I hope this letter finds you well. I'm an enjoyer of your memoir, and have learned a great deal about the Paloma from your site. I appreciated your note on historiography last month!

I am a doctoral candidate and researcher at the University of Leeds, and have been working on a dissertation about vaudeville in the 20s-30s—specifically on the business lives of vaudevillian women. I was wondering if, in the course of your research, you've found documents concerning Paloma Gallo? She seems to have been quite important to the club's establishment. To your knowledge, are there records of her after 1928?

Thanks so much; any help is appreciated!

Sincerely,

Emily McDougal

* * *

Dear Miss McDougal,

Thank you for your interest. I am heartened that your dissertation may touch on Paloma Gallo, and am glad the blog has been of use to you.

In my searches of the Brighton archives, I have found only the attached palladiotype photographs of Gallo. (Looks rather like Theda Bara, doesn't she?) Sadly, her brush with Allgyer seems also to have been her only brush with the historical record. Some earlier ephemera from the 1910s, in the form of a Southampton vaudeville program, mention a singer named Maria Gallo and 'songs by the same.' This may be our Paloma, through who knows. She does not appear in any news or records after her split from Allgyer.

The records I do have (mostly retellings of the story in brochures provided by Paloma staff, plus the aforementioned unverified programs) are attached. Additionally, I add some legal documents concerning Allgyer—she was wise to leave him, given his conduct towards future wives.

My sincere best wishes for your research, and do let me know if you find anything more.

xxxx -LD

* * *

ET IN PALOMA
(Kaur, ctd)

The thing is pale, and grey. At first, I can't see what it is, or why Tover is avoiding it, pulling his legs up onto the banister and shouting as it buoys up against his legs. He reaches back for me, and pulls me to the side. The thing slides out, emerging from the stairs and bobbing next to us.

I turn the torch on it. At first I think it is another mat of fungus, or a prop. Ropy, black stuff spreads out around it; only slowly do I realize that this substance is hair. It issues from a bulge of grey that sits atop the larger mass and bears the rough proportions of a head. Two sunken indents, two little puckered slits. Below all that, a froglike orifice: it has five yellow teeth, all extending outwards at perverse angles. Gasping, impossibly wide, sucking at the dark air as though feeding endlessly.

I help pull Tover upright, and he staggers up the rest of the stairs. I keep the beam trained on the mass. My mind seems to detach from me, keeps operating while I passively receive its input, none of which I'm not ready for: it's a corpse, a human body with the proportions all wrong, and it is floating like Ophelia through fake hibiscus.

* * *

'LOVE IS STRANGE INDEED' (1965)
I see my baby comin'
Her love is strange indeed
Who knows where it comes from
Or what it can see

Maybe I'll know someday
If I pray and I dream it
Til then I just follow
Her music and sing it [...]

* * *

FORENSIC STUDY OF SAPONIFIED HUMAN REMAINS
FOUND IN A BRIGHTON SITE (Abstract)

[...] Archeological investigation of the site indicates that the body was concealed 70 to 80 years ago, in a shallow grave covered with quick-drying cement. Over the ensuing decades, moisture from the water table gradually wore down the cement barrier, which was broken open during a recent collapse of the building's foundations.

Within the sealed grave, moist conditions accelerated the conversion of key tissues into adipocere, especially in heavy whitish concentrations on the hands and midsection. Post-mortem examinations revealed that internal organs were shrunken but well-preserved.

Due to the nature of concealment, foul play was likely involved, though precise cause of death cannot be determined. While the precise date of death is currently unknown, investigations of the body and fabric matter have revealed two metal buttons stamped with the date 1925, indicating the deceased was likely interred in the decade afterward.

DNA studies of the hair were inconclusive, due to the hair's degraded quality. Possible genetic markers of Italian and Eastern European ancestry may be present. Researchers from the University of Surrey are conducting further analysis from different samples.

* * *

PALOMA: BRIGHT LIGHTS, VICE, AND MUSIC
(Dinn, p. 305)

What shall we make of the Lady? I have been asked this many times, and respond thus: I do not think it is for us to make anything of her. In fact, I feel deeply that the opposite is true.

Sometimes I imagine her down there, in her empire of stillness, and wonder whether all of us above in the Paloma had been dreaming at her pleasure, passing through flickering images and sounds, going about our little trysts and fetes... while she has been awake below, enduring, waiting.

It is not pleasant to approach the borders of the dream that we call life. One feels a sudden coldness, lies awake at night to the sensations of earth and suffocation. Most of us turn our minds away. Some are drawn deeper, for whatever reason.

Often I miss the folk I knew in those old days. I imagine some bright future that will make the pain sting less. But I stop myself. Because I know—perhaps through the instruction of Lane Britton—that there really is no such thing as the future: just an endless past that will keep going after we are gone.

* * *

'SWEET TEETH' (1972)
[...] Drag me to the place
Where my mind hasn't been
I've done you wrong
I won't do it again (yeah)
All the girls that I see
Just remind me of you (3×)
Don't stop until
I'm part of you

The Daybreak Killer

Inspired by *Daybreak* from the album
This One's for You (1976)

Matt McGee

An attractive young woman in her mid-30's lay dead on the worn Formica of a Los Angeles club called the Flamenco. Locals mostly called it The Flamingo because the exterior was a pale shade of Miami pink and a large date palm stood beside its door.

The woman had fallen beneath the fake green leaves of a fake green tree selected for its vaguely tropical appearance. Poked into its faux soil, like the other twenty-eight fake trees around the room were two plastic flamingoes. If the owners of The Flamenco were trying to encourage people to get the name of their bar right, they weren't trying very hard.

A senior detective named Parmenter crouched beside the woman, pencil in one hand and a small notebook in the other. His partner, a younger man named Bernal, stepped up behind him.

"What's her name?" Bernal asked.

"Owner of the Flamenco, whose name I wrote down here, said it's Lola."

"You're kidding. And let me guess, she was a show girl?

"Waitress. Showgirl?"

Bernal pointed at the yellow feathers clipped in her hair.

"Yeah, not a whole lot of people wear those anymore."

"What's Lola's last name?"

"Schwartz."

Bernal crunched his brow. "Lola Schwartz, that's her name?"

"What's wrong with that?"

"Nothing. Just not what I expected I guess. So what happened to ol' Lola? And don't say 'then the punches flew, tables were smashed in two.'"

The elder looked at his partner incredulously. "Why not?"

"You're not getting any of this, are you? Jesus, what kind of music were you raised on anyway?"

Parmenter shrugged. "Mostly the Beatles."

"OK, well at least that's respectable."

"Respectable?"

"Yeah. Either way, when we get back in the car I need to play some things for you."

"Such as?"

"Such as *Manilow II.*"

"You know, half the time I don't know what you're talking about and this is definitely one of those times."

"Let's just get Lola here tagged and bagged and collect our evidence OK?"

"Fine."

"Fine," Bernal said. "But I already know who did it."

"Who?"

"His name is Rico. And here's what happened."

Parmenter waited.

"So his name was Rico. He called her over. Shit! I can't remember the rest of it!"

"Again, no idea what you're talking about."

"You'll understand when we get in the car."

Bernal started away from the scene, whistling as he went. The older detective didn't know the song, but he had to admit the tune sounded familiar.

* * *

That afternoon, Parmenter huddled over his desk, scribbling into paperwork when Bernal walked in.

"Got the reports here on our girl Schwartz," Parmenter said.

"Lola?"

"Yeah well, we were all a little off on that one. Her name isn't Lola, it's Melanie."

"Natural mistake, what with the yellow feather in her hair—"

"And the dress cut down to there, right. I've heard the song now. Anyway, coroner believes she was killed right around 5:45 in the morning."

"That makes our killer an early riser. Or late worker."

"Coroner also said that cause of death was strangulation. Said our guy, or girl, was a pretty big one. Estimated height between six-two and six-six, weight over two-twenty. Large hands."

"DNA?"

"Too early to know."

"So maybe we can dig up some profiles, work something up on big and tall suspects?"

Parmenter nodded.

"Or hit up the big and tall men's stores," Bernal added.

"Might not be a bad idea."

"Thanks. Either way, one thing's for sure."

"What's that?"

"We got a suspect at large."

Parmenter sighed. "Why do you do that?"

"It's like an itch I have to scratch."

"Someday when you become a father all those jokes are going to come in handy."

"I'm counting on it."

"But for now they're just annoying."

Bernal shrugged.

"You know what else is annoying," Parmenter added, "that I haven't eaten anything today. Let's talk about this over lunch."

"Cool."

"Ideas?"

"On lunch? You pick. I owe you for the "at-large" joke."

"If you call that a joke."

* * *

Parmenter and Bernal walked into Carl's jr Charbroiler, their eyes on the overhead menu. Parmenter's gaze drifted down to the young man behind the counter; tall, heavy, and leaned over the register with a hand on each side.

Parmenter leaned toward his junior partner. "You see the size of this guy?"

"Yeah."

"How tall would you say he is?"

"Don't know. Probably six-two if he stands up straight."

"I'm going with six-four at least. What do you say he weighs?"

"Probably about 220."

"You're being generous, that boy ain't that svelte. I'm going with 260."

"So what's your interest all of a sudden in," Bernal squinted at the guy's name tag, "Victor?"

"Well, I'd say he's a little too big to work at Carl's Jr. wouldn't ya think?"

"Too big as in too old?"

"No, too big as in BIG. His natural talents are going to waste in a place like this."

"Not if the manager sees his natural talents as an asset."

"How so."

"Maybe he sees ol' Victor there can change lightbulbs and lift heavy stuff off the delivery truck other people would usually shy away from."

"Got a point."

"Yes I do. Manager probably always schedules ol' Victor there for the hours when the delivery guy happens to show up. Has him toting those boxes—"

"Lifting that bale," Bernal said.

"Exactly. What's more, if ol Victor there is working the night shift..."

"It's 5:23 now…"

"If ol' Victor there's working the night shift he's got all night to stalk his prey, catch it, and get back in time for his late shift after a good night's sleep."

"Gentlemen may I take your order?"

The two eyed Victor. "Yes Victor, you can."

Victor had seen them come in but, like a lot of overworked fast food employees he'd quickly left his initial station and marched from one unmanned post to another. He handed bags of food out the drive-thru window, tapped on a series of tablets tied to delivery apps and monitored the clock for his own benefit. When he returned to his register station, he leaned forward and kept both hands on the register as if he were under arrest and subconsciously assuming the position.

"So Victor, how's it going today?"

No answer, just a shrug and a groan.

Parmenter never took his eyes off the overhead menu. "Well Victor I think I'm gonna have the Western Bacon Cheeseburger."

"Make that a combo?"

"Sure Victor, I don't give a shit about my heart. Who does?"

Victor mumbled something that sounded like a whole, quick sentence.

"What was that?"

"I said 'I'm a vegetarian.'"

"And you work *here*?"

"Ain't easy." Victor pointed up. "Worst part's that fucking music. I come home smelling like seared flesh with Paul fucking Anka in my head."

"Every job's got a downside, Victor. Gotta work and earn money somewhere."

Another grunt and shrug, then Victor's eyes turned toward Bernal. "For you sir?"

"Me? Oh, nothing. Not hungry. I'm a vegetarian too, Victor."

Parmenter crunched his brow. "You are?"

"Yep."

"Since when?"

"Since years ago. Dated a vegetarian and she kinda talked me into it."

"But you're broken up now?"

"Yeah."

"Well I'd say the coast is clear and you're free to eat whatever the hell you want."

"You're right. Victor, I'll have what he's having. Supersize it. I don't give a shit about my heart either. And one more thing."

Victor typed, tapped at the register. "Yeah what's that."

"You're kind of a tall drink of water, Victor. Exactly how tall are you?"

"Six-four."

"That's if you stand up straight, right?"

At Bernal's suggestion Victor stood up straight.

"Damn. And how much do you weigh Victor."

"Why?"

"Just a little wager between my friend and I. I'd said you were two-twenty and he said 'no way.' So…"

"Two-sixty-two this morning."

"Damn, we were both wrong! Weigh yourself every morning Victor?"

"What's with all the questions?"

"We're just curious about—"

"'Cause you sound like my damn Dad. Besides most people who ask about my size are usually women. Who are you guys?"

"Just a couple guys in need of Western Bacon Cheeseburger combos, Victor. Here's my card."

"You guys talk like cops."

Bernal pointed at his partner. "He gets that all the time. Weren't you just telling me the other day people are always saying you look and sound like a cop?"

"It's true, people are always saying that to me. Wish I had a cop's retirement package."

Bernal shook his head. "Those guys make out like fucking bandits don't they?"

"That's what I hear. Some make full salary for years after they retire."

"That's pretty fucking sweet. How about you Victor? You got your retirement package all picked out?"

"We only have 401k."

"Well that's a start, eh Victor? You start saving now you could retire at, what," he looked at his partner, "seventy-six."

"Eighty. But by then he'd already be old and infirm. See, guys here that are Victor's size…"

Victor had produced a couple jumbo plastic cups and set them down with a bit more force than necessary, though it might've been just right to send a message.

"Sorry Victor were we bugging you?"

"We didn't mean to."

"We really didn't. I mean, my buddy here can be a real pain in the ass but that's just because he's dealing with his girlfriend the vegetarian…"

"Ex."

"Right, his ex-girlfriend the vegetarian and he just needs a good meal and probably a prostitute or two."

Victor turned, took a paper bag from a well-stocked pile, flicked his wrist and popped it open. His back stayed turned to the two.

Parmenter frowned. "You've upset Victor."

"Me? You're the bad cop in this situation."

"Let's get a table. Victor needs to get back to work."

Parmenter strode across the empty restaurant and slid into a table in the furthest corner. "Kinda got the place to ourselves."

Bernal sat down. "Alright," he said, "where are we on suspects?"

"Ran the height and weight through the computer and came up with eight possibles. Four are currently incarcerated."

"Always a perfect alibi."

"Of the other four, three also have alibis that check out and the fourth, well he's airtight."

"Airtight because…"

"He's dead."

"Another great alibi. So where's that leave us?"

"Up a creek momentarily. But I was thinking about your idea earlier."

"About Rico?"

"Knock it off with the 'Copacabana' references already. No, I was thinking—"

"Gentlemen your food is ready."

Bernal looked up; Victor towered at the order-up window. He spun a tray their direction.

"You liking Victor there a little more? Hey Victor, where were you this morning around 5:45?"

He watched Bernal approach. "Probably asleep."

"Got any witnesses to that?"

"About forty."

"You realize that doesn't make any sense, right Victor."

"Actually it makes a lot of sense if you know what Only Fans is." Victor tossed some ketchup packets on the tray. He turned and walked away.

Bernal returned with the tray, set it on the table and slid the seat of his pants across the bench seat. "What's Only Fans?"

"What?!"

"Only Fans. Victor there says his alibi is that he was asleep but then added something about having forty witnesses through something called Only Fans."

"Jesus, he would." Parmenter quickly explained that Only Fans was a chance for people to watch you do your normal daily routines at home via webcam.

"And people pay for this stupid shit?"

Parmenter nodded. "Considering your age I'm surprised this is news to you."

"That's gotta be the dumbest thing I've ever heard. Who would pay good money to watch a giant guy like that sleep?"

"Fans of pro wrestlers? I don't know. Everyone's got a physical type that turns them on and I guess ol' Victor there is someone's side of beef. But to be fair, just so you know, it's usually hot girls that have the accounts."

"Hot girls will pay to watch Victor sleep?!"

"How did you make detective? No. Usually the hot girls have the web cams and you watch them do stuff."

Bernal shook his head. "OK well, I guess I understand it a little better that way. But really, who wants to pay to watch someone do their laundry or clean the oven?"

"Not me. Got better things to spend my money on."

"Same. OK well, before we got distracted by Victor's web cam over there, you were saying something about my having had a great idea."

Parmenter chewed a few fries. "It wasn't a great idea per se, but you mentioned earlier about the Big & Tall mens store. Might pay off to go in and talk to the owner."

"Have we got a Big and Tall store around here?"

Parmenter drew his cell from his suit coat pocket, typed in the passcode and lit the screen. "Four actually. One is just a tailor shop, two are regular clothing stores, Ross and Goodwill if you can believe that, who say they carry things that bigger and taller people might consider a find. Then there's Gary's XL."

"Is it owned by an actual Gary?"

Parmenter nodded. "An actual Gary. Used to be an actor. So it says in the bio, and apparently he had trouble getting jobs because the wardrobe people rarely had anything his size. They'd ix-nay on his being ast-cay. Guessing he still blames them for submarining his shot at fame and fortune."

"So he started his own shop."

"Yep."

Bernal nodded. "Sounds like Gary could be a suspect in Lola's slaying. Missed his chance at fortune and fame and took it out on Lola the show girl."

"Melanie. And she was a waitress."

Bernal looked back toward the front counter. Victor lumbered station to station. He leaned on the bagging station while his cook assembled the latest burgers.

"I still like the big guy over there."

"If you like him that much, subscribe to his Only Fans page. Meanwhile, finish up your burger. We've gotta go check out Gary's."

* * *

They rode down the 101 freeway to the Topanga Canyon exit and headed north. Once a sign of out-of-control development, the aging strip mall had given way to taller, shinier buildings in all directions. A long rectangular sign announced Gary's XL in plain block red letters.

The interior was adorned with photos of bigger, taller and heavier clients who'd patronized Gary's over the decades. A few recognizable actors, a professional wrestler, two former NFL players. And in every photo, beside the celebrity client of honor was the same tall man.

"Gentlemen," a sultry female voice said.

The woman who had appeared with the sound of the door's cowbell was nearing middle aged and wearing it well. Brunette, high-wattage smile, clad in a vintage dress that did her modest curves justice, and her step sounded with a pair of Rodeo's best Italian leather. She tilted her chin to just the right angle so the sunlight set off her already rugged cheekbones.

"I'm Mandy, how may I help you two today?"

"Mandy," Bernal mumbled, "of course." He took the unusual step of approaching with a shield gleaming in his wallet. "We'd like to speak with Gary."

The high-wattage smile never dimmed and Mandy gave a mild nod. "Just a moment, I'll see if he's off the phone."

Mandy disappeared through the kind of swinging doors common to old western saloons. A man with longer, thick gray-hair at a desk turned Mandy's way, listened, then rose to his feet.

And rose and rose. Gary seemed to unfold away from his desk like a praying mantis. He leaned through the swinging doors.

"Officers, how may I help you?"

"Mr. Maxwell?"

"Yes."

"I'm Detective Bernal and this is my partner Detective Parmenter."

"Nice to meet you both. Judging by your sizes, I'm guessing you're not in the market for a new wardrobe."

"No," Parmenter said, "but we know a few guys in our department who could use your services."

Gary plucked a card from a small plastic rack. "Send them. Always ready to help law enforcement. And yes, there is a discount."

"We'll pass this on. Mr Maxwell, we're investigating a homicide."

"Wow. Mandy would you excuse us?"

Mandy moved toward the swinging doors.

"Actually Mandy," Bernal said, "perhaps you could be of help as well."

Mandy turned and stayed. The high-wattage smile brightened.

"There was a murder committed by a larger man, over six-two, likely in excess of two-hundred and twenty pounds."

"Uh-oh," Mandy turned to her boss, "you're a suspect!"

Gary put up his hands the way he might've seen in a favorite old movie. "I didn't do it!"

"We don't have you on the suspect list," Parmenter said.

"Yet," Bernal added.

"But just to be sure, where were you this morning around 5:45?"

"Yum-Yum."

Bernal and Parmenter looked at each other. "Sorry?"

"It's a donut store in Agoura Hills, near my house. I'm up and doing at five. Walk the dog, dress, shower, then head down to Yum-Yum on

Kanan Road for an oat bran muffin. And orange juice. They make it fresh. I'm here around 6:15'ish, depending on traffic. Disarm the alarm, get to work."

"I'm usually here around eight," Mandy offered.

"Thank you. We'd like to know is if you've got any customers you can think of off the top of your heads that are… suspicious."

"Suspicious how," Gary asked.

"Angry. Potentially violent. Anyone who might strike you as the powder keg type."

Gary and Mandy's eyes drifted away, scanning internal data bases. Slowly, both shook their heads. "None come to mind right away," Gary said. "Most of our customers are pretty appreciative. You know, since a big or tall man can't just walk into Nordstrom's and pick something off the rack. They come to us and we cater to their specific needs. Not to brag but they usually leave pretty happy."

"So no one who's left *un*happy as of late."

Again, the shake of heads. "Nope," Gary said.

"How about relatives."

"How do you mean?"

"With bigger and taller the size DNA usually doesn't fall too far from the tree. Has anyone come in recently whose son or daughter has been in trouble with the law lately?"

Mandy pointed at Gary. "There's that guy, Smitty."

Parmenter and Bernal listened.

"Smitty," Gary seemed to forget.

"The guy with the blue pickup? Gray hair, has the friendly dog."

"Oh. Right, Smitty. What about him?"

"Last time he was in, boy, he must've gone on for fifteen or twenty minutes about how his son was in trouble with one thing or another. Smitty said he had to kick him out. Change the locks on the doors."

"He didn't mention it to me."

"You were at the bank last time he came in. Bought a couple shirts."

"Would you have any information on file about this Smitty or his son?"

"Actually yes," Gary said. "Smitty's an old customer, dating back to when we still kept paper files. If you'll wait, I'll go pull what I have and photocopy it. It'll take just a moment."

"We appreciate it."

Gary went through the swinging doors.

"Mandy," Parmenter said, "did he happen to mention the name of his son?"

Her eyes slid slowly away. "Sorry. I don't remember it if he did."

"Has he ever been a customer here?"

"The son?"

"Yes."

Mandy shook her head. "Never met him. Judging by the stories Smitty told I'd say the kid was likely late teens, early twenties."

"Thank you. You've been very helpful."

"I hope they're both alright," Mandy said.

"We'll check it out."

Gary returned through the swinging doors holding a single sheet of paper. "Copy of a receipt from 2014. Real name's Steve Smith. Receipt has his full name, home address, phone number. Far as I know he hasn't moved or changed his info. Hope it helps."

"Thanks Mr. Maxwell, we appreciate the help."

"Anything to help an investigation. And I hope Smitty's not in too much trouble this time."

"This time?" Parmenter asked.

Gary gave a little shrug. "I don't want to speak ill of anyone, especially a good paying customer that appreciates what we do here."

"But," Bernal said.

"But Smitty," Gary grimaced, "to be blunt, Smitty's one of those guys."

"One of what guys."

"A shit magnet. You've known the type. Like trouble is the norm rather than the exception. And when things aren't going sideways, they go out and find trouble where there might not be any."

"We know the type."

"In your business I'm sure you do. Another thing about Smitty," Gary added.

"What's that."

"Always has money. Not the kind who's looking for a bargain. Usually pays cash too."

"Well," Parmenter said, "sometimes their type run into trouble too."

* * *

Bernal and Parmenter were on their way back over the hill toward town when Bernal's cell rang. He looked at the screen then leaned it where Parmenter could see it.

"Boss calling."

"Probably just checking our progress."

Bernal picked up. "Andy's Undergarments where every panty is a perfect fit, how may I—"

"Is everything a goddamn JOKE to you?"

Bernal drew his ear away. When the coast sounded clear he brought the phone back.

"Actually boss we're making some good headway. We interviewed—"

"I don't care if you interviewed the Pope. You two have got another killing on your hands."

Bernal put the call on speaker. "Where's the body, chief?"

"Little park over off Laro Street called Sumac. Female, mid-thirties. Lady walking her dog discovered her around seven in the morning."

"Another early morning killing."

"Starting to look that way. Now look, smartass. We've got real trouble. Not just a second killing but now the media's gotten a hold of the story. And they've got a name for it: 'The Daybreak Killer.'"

"Oh Jesus. Another Barry Manilow tie-in."

"What?"

"It's a song," Bernal said. He repeated the name aloud as if trying it on for size. "The Daybreak Killer.' Not sure I like it much but it'll probably get hits online."

"Which in my day we used to call 'selling copy.' A reporter gets hold of something like this and runs it into the ground. The public gets freaked out thinking this guy's lurking in the bushes everywhere and pretty soon they're yelling at the cops 'do something, do something, protect and serve!'"

"Like we're not already doing that," Bernal said. "We'll go straight to Sumac. Who's running the scene?"

"One of the Lost Hills sheriffs guys, name of Kronkite. No relation."

"To who," Bernal said.

"Jesus, I forget how young you are. Preliminary investigation says the MO's the same. Big guy, strangulation."

"We're on it, chief." Bernal hung up. "You believe this? Now we've got The Daybreak Killer to add to the city's history. We better clear this up fast."

"Call Records about this Smitty guy," Parmenter said, "see if he's got a package. Son as well."

"Got it." Bernal dialed his cell.

"This new body at Sumac could be a break for us."

How?"

Parmenter took the Kanan Road off-ramp. "Sooner or later this guy's gonna slip. And when he does…"

"We're gonna be right there," Bernal said.

* * *

The woman's body lay in the center of Sumac Park near a large playground. She'd worn a button-down cardigan to beat the morning chill.

Parmenter bounced the SUV into the parking spaces affront the park among four patrol units. They gave their names and badges to a female officer with a clipboard.

"That way gentlemen," she pointed her pen toward a group of officers. Parmenter and Bernal approached. Introductions were made.

"So, what've we got?"

"Strangulation," the deputy named Kronkite said. "Body was dumped. Didn't happen here."

"So we've gotta guess where it did happen and why."

"Roger that."

Parmenter wandered to where yellow tape was strung around mature, fully grown trees.

"Deceased got a name?" Bernal asked.

"Miffy," Kronkite announced. "Short for Millicent, aka Milly. She went by Miffy though, that's what's on her driver's licence. Age thirty-one. Last known occupation, bank teller."

"Where at?"

"Wells Fargo," Kronkite pointed his pencil, "one right here by Rite Aid."

Bernal crunched a brow. "By the Carl's jr?"

Kronkite nodded. "That's the one."

Bernal's glanced toward Parmenter, who was examining a large nearby tree.

"Hey partner," Parmenter waved, "c'mere."

Bernal approached. The sun was reaching its golden hour. Parmenter pointed down at a small, weathered plaque.

"What is it?" Bernal asked.

"See the name there?"

Bernal crouched closer. "Who's Ron Goldman?"

Parmenter sighed. "Did you study *anything* at the academy?"

Bernal shrugged. "Saw the movies. Thought I was gonna be partners with Hightower and getting chased around a desk by that blonde, Whatshername."

"Kim Cattrall."

"Yeah. Didn't work out."

"You ever see the *Naked Gun* movies?"

"One. Had OJ Simpson in it, right?"

Parmenter pointed at the plaque. "That guy was killed by OJ."

Bernal hooked a thumb at the plaque. "That your personal opinion?"

"He was killed by OJ. Now, forgetting that a moment, do you think it's a coincidence that our girl over there was dumped near this plaque?"

"It's a stretch."

"Or an homage," Parmenter said. "Messed up people do messed up things."

"Detectives," Kronkite called. "Got something."

Parmenter and Bernal returned. A CSI tech drew an item from the pocket of the woman's cardigan: a single-serving ketchup packet.

"How much you wanna bet that packet has a smiling yellow star on it," Parmenter said.

"Wouldn't take that bet."

Bernal's cell rang. He looked at the stored number. "It's Records."

He stepped away to take the call. Parmenter looked down at the plaque. As a slight evening breeze rustled his hair he thought of a handsome young man who'd had a job waiting tables, had gone to return a pair of sunglasses and paid the highest price.

"Hey partner," Bernal announced, "let's roll."

Parmenter shook back to reality. "What's up."

"Need to swing by Carl's," Bernal said.

"Not hungry."

"Doesn't matter. That Smitty guy? Mandy was right. Got quite a record. You know what else he's got?"

Parmenter waited.

"A son named Victor."

Parmenter climbed behind the wheel. "Let's go."

"See," Bernal said, "I told you, cop's instinct, man. Only Fans my ass!"

* * *

Victor was behind the counter when Bernal and Parmenter pulled in. Maybe it was the swiftness of how the detective's car swung into the lot, but as Victor watched the two walk in, he lifted his hands lightly and said "OK, I'm not running."

Bernal took out a set of cuffs and drew Victor's arms behind him.

"Not running from what Victor?"

"You're here about that bank teller, whatshername."

"That whatshername had a name Victor, it was Miffy."

"God what a stupid goddamn name. She deserved it."

Parmenter raised a brow. "Why the park, Victor."

"Sacrifice," Victor said.

"You kidding?"

"No, I'm not kidding you dumbass. You don't get it."

Bernal lead Victor around the counter and out the front door, into the last rays of the day's sunshine. "No I don't Victor. But I'll get you something at the station you can sign that'll tell us all about it."

* * *

"So what'd Victor say?"

Parmenter closed the file with the printed version of Victor's statement. "Climbed in bed with the camera on, rolled out the other side with pillows in his place. Killed Melanie and Miffy and drove them to the dump spots. Says the music made him do it. His victims were customers who'd come in and enjoyed the piped in tunes. Miffy had been shaking her hips to 'Mr Telephone Man.'"

"New Edition?!"

"Guess so. I've heard the song and always thought it was the Jackson Five. Our girl Melanie, aka Lola…"

"Who was a showgirl…"

"She wasn't a showgirl. Victor caught her singing along to Richard Marx."

Bernal shrugged. "OK, that might be murder-worthy."

"I know you're kidding. It's the old Son of Sam defense. 'The dog made me do it.' Victor is already claiming insanity by means of being pummeled with easy listening."

Bernal sat and kicked his feet up on his desk, folded his hands over his tight belly. "If you could choose the last song you hear before you die, what would it be?"

Parmenter drifted into thought, then smiled. "Told you I was raised on The Beatles. So for me? 'Nowhere Man.'"

"Seems kinda maudlin."

Parmenter shrugged. "Seems like that's what we deal with day in and day out here. People making great plans no one will ever follow through. How about you?"

Bernal shook his head. "Don't have one."

"What?"

"Music's not that important to me. I mean, I love certain bands, songs, but my opinions aren't that strong. Nothing I'd kill over anyway. You know?"

Parmenter nodded. "Yeah," he said. "Unfortunately not everyone feels that way."

A Connecticut Stalker

Inspired by *Weekend in New England* from the album
This One's for You (1976)

Laurie Stevens

Inbox

From: YourFriend [YourFriend@x_raydius-mail.com]
To: NoahW [w.noah@glcuco.com]
Date: September 22, 6:53 PM
Subject: A Proposition

Hi. It's me. I won't write my name because of the restraining order, but you know who it is. It's *me*. The email address above is fake, but you wouldn't have opened it if you knew it came from me.

All I can think about is our precious weekend in Rowayton, how we walked along the beach together and gazed at the boats on the water. Don't you remember how romantic that was? The sun glowed orange on the horizon and turned the water pink. I held onto your arm as we talked. Why are you ghosting me?

I tell nearly everyone I meet about the day we met. I'd left work in Norwalk and drove over to hang out near those fancy houses on the shoreline. Rowayton is so beautiful, green, and stately. Can you imagine what it would be like to live in one of those mansions and have a view of the water? Of course, you can imagine it. Your family lives in one of those homes!

To be honest, before we met, I sort of hung outside a couple of those places– just to see who lived in them. I wasn't spying or anything like that, just observing. Want to hear something dope? I actually approached one guy about six months ago. He looked to be in his late twenties and was really cute. I pretended I had car trouble and asked him for help. I asked if I could use his iPhone to "call" for a tow. Then, I went into his settings and memorized his phone number. Of course, I never called for the tow. I just pretended I did. He gave me his first name – Troy. Maybe you know him? I already knew his last name because I peeked into his mailbox. I tried contacting him many times, but he turned out to be a real jerk. That doesn't matter anymore. We're talking about you and me now.

Remember how I stumbled over a rock on the beach, and you ran over to see if I was okay? I can't stop thinking about the feel of your strong hand on my arm as you helped me up. I can still see your brown hair ruffling in the sea breeze. The way you pushed your curls out of your eyes and asked if I was okay. You wore a light blue shirt that day and beige shorts. God, I noticed your hot legs right away, including that tiny tattoo of a half-moon, which looks soooo sexy on your ankle. And then, when I kept stumbling around like a klutz and asked if I could hold onto you, you were nice enough to give me your arm.

Honestly, there are no guys like you out there. Trust me, I know. Hinge and Tinder and all those dating sites. Meh. Useless. Those sites offer an endless supply of fratty boys. Children. Not like you, Noah. I repeat: there are no other guys like you.

Hee-hee. I keep thinking about that strong hand of yours. I keep thinking that I'd like you to put it on my bod, but don't get all weirded out. I'm fine taking things slow.

Remember when I invited you to a clambake the night we met, and you said, "I have a girlfriend." I know you were just scared. Serious relationships are intimidating, but Noah, you don't have to be scared of me.

Honestly, there was no clambake. I just said that to see if you would go. Can you imagine me at one of those boujee parties? Me, with my frizzy bleached hair and neon pink beanie. Me, with my klutzy, big-boned body. I'd probably stumble right into the firepit and send all those lobster tails and mussels flying. I seriously doubt I'd ever get invited to some snooty clambake on the beach. You and me… We don't need those kinds of snobs.

We're soulmates, Noah.

You were on the beach alone that day looking for REAL love, just like me. Now, don't repeat that you were there just to catch a sunset view. YOU came over to ME. I didn't come to you.

Yes, I asked to use your cell phone to get your number, which was sneaky, but you MUST have known I would do that. You let me have your phone, after all. You secretly wanted me to have your number. You know that. I know that.

Then, when I started calling and texting you, you insisted that you only walked over to me that day to see if I was okay, that you saw me fall on the rocks, and only wanted to be a good Samaritan.

But I know better. There's a cosmic string tying us together, Noah. I have a sense for such things. I have special abilities, you know. I'm unique. Remember when you tried to put me off by asking me not to call you anymore? You even tried to insult me by saying my high-pitched giggling annoys you. I could tell you were nervous. Your voice did crack on a couple of occasions when we spoke over the phone. You felt too shy to express your love for me. You don't understand the cosmic string, but I do because I have special abilities. Unfortunately, my abilities don't extend to turning on other people's cell phones, so would you please take my damn calls? Talk about annoying.

Being apart is driving me crazy. I told you our paths wouldn't have crossed unless we were meant for each other. I want to hold you. When can I hold you? All I have is the memory of your hand on my arm. When can I touch you again? Noah, this separation isn't good for our relationship.

I did some searching on Google and found your email address. I also found out where you go to college. I didn't know you go to NYU. I was in nursing school in Fairfield for a while but dropped out. Well, I kind of got expelled. They said I was mean to the patients, but that's a lot of bull. I mean, some people are obnoxious, you know? So what if I didn't give them their medications on time? I was watching TikTok. That shit's addicting, you know? It's not that I don't want to be a nurse. I do. I just can't take whiny people.

Anyhow, enough about me. I bought a new dress, and it's really sexy. I imagine walking into a hotel room at one of those exotic resorts and seeing you waiting for me on the bed. You know the kind of resort I'm talking about. Palm trees on the sand. Sparkling ocean water. A trip like that would remind us of our weekend together.

You would LOVE me in this dress. Did I tell you I made a reservation for us at a resort hotel in the Bahamas? Yeah, at Resorts World in Bimini. Look it up. I'm trying to be proactive and take the bull by the horns, so to speak. You're not doing anything to help our relationship, that's for sure. I tried calling you to tell you about the reservation, but you won't take my calls. Apparently, you've BLOCKED my number. How are we supposed to talk to each other if you block my number?

That was a low blow, Noah. Now, I can't send you pictures of myself anymore. Didn't you like getting my sexy shots? I may not have the best body in the world, but you didn't have to ignore me. I'm what they call athletic, okay? Broad shoulders, big-boned. *Athletic.* Then, I found out you blocked me on all your social media accounts. Why did you do that? I couldn't tag you in posts anymore.

Why are you making this so hard on us? I have no choice but to email you like some rando salesperson, and it really sucks corresponding this way. You are the love of my life. And that restraining order! You claim I'm trying to ruin your life. Well, you're ruining mine! We had a *relationship.* It might have been brief, but it was pretty fricking powerful. I felt it. You felt it. Why are you doing this?

We need to meet. When will I see you again? It's been weeks.

Inbox

From: YourFriend [YourFriend@x_raydius-mail.com]
To: NoahW[w.noah@glcuco.com]
Date: September 22, 7:46 PM

Subject: RE: A Proposition

I cut my hair. It's short now. It's still bleached but short. Why did I cut it? I had to. I didn't know that if you don't wash your hair for a while, you get, like, dreadlocks…? I don't know why I didn't wash my hair. Maybe I forgot to shower. I can't think about these things. I've been thinking about YOU too much.

Help me, Noah. Help me make this strong yearning end. I don't always connect well with people. I don't care about most people. I don't have patience for idiots. I admit that most people bring out the worst in me.

But not you. Don't you get it? With you, I can bring out all the love that I have. With you, I'm in heaven. I don't understand why you would want to avoid me.

Here's another thing. I forgot to pay my rent. Now, my landlord is threatening to evict me. See what you've done? If I didn't have to concentrate on us so much, I'd be able to be normal. Instead, I'm a wreck.

I'm two in love with you. It kills me that I want to bare my soul to you, and you ignore me. Sometimes, I get so sick and frustrated I sit in my apartment and eat Jack in the Box tacos, one right after the other. Those tacos are super cheap, and I have to be careful because I'm in between jobs.

That's right. I lost my job because of you. I couldn't concentrate at work. All those whiners with chronic kidney disease drove me crazy. Honestly, how can I make someone with end-stage renal failure feel better when I feel like dying myself? It's not fair. I guess my boss wondered why I haven't been showing up for work. How can I explain that I've been busy trying to save my relationship with you?

I'M NOT ANGRY with you for making me lose my job, although I don't know how I'm going to pay my rent without an income. Again, I'M NOT ANGRY. Being a Patient Care Technician at a dialysis clinic isn't very glamorous. As you know, I wanted to be an RN. The job was a step down for me, so I don't care that I was fired. I have more important things to consider now like trips to Bimini with my handsome boyfriend. ☺ ♥ ♥ ♥

Noah, we started a story whose end has to wait. Why? Why wait? Why bury our love? Why are you avoiding me? Why would you file a restraining order against the woman in your life? I'm your soulmate.

This is so upsetting. Is it that skank you're hanging around with? I happen to know that the student slut you call your girlfriend is not suitable for you. I've been following her around and can tell she's not right for you. I went to your school and watched her. She's so basic, Noah. She's way beneath you. What's her name again? Trixie? Dixie? Ashley. That's her name. Ass-Lee. Smash-Lee. What a ditz. Chatting with her "besties" (fellow beasties), flipping her long, dark hair over her shoulder like she doesn't have a care in the world. Her smooth skin, her manicured nails, her beautiful body—she makes me sick. I'd like to shove her down a manhole.

Inbox

From: YourFriend [YourFriend@x_ray-mail.com]
To: NoahW[w.noah@glcuco.com]
Date: September 22, 8:12 PM
Subject: RE: A Proposition

You're in college, but I'm in my early thirties, which means I know what's better for you. I'm the mature one; you're the baby. You should listen to me.

I followed you around campus, too. You didn't see me, of course. I wore a backpack and a different beanie and blended in. One time, you looked my way, and I almost had a heart attack. I ducked behind a bush, scared that you would catch me. You chewed your lip and seemed nervous as you looked around. Did you sense my presence? I think you did. That's the cosmic string tying us together. I'll bet if I tried, I could read your thoughts.

I have to tell you, watching you while you were unaware was exhilarating. I felt powerful, in control of you. For that moment, I owned you, and it felt good. Really good. I could fantasize about you, knowing you were less than a few yards away. If only my fantasy could reach out, grab you, and pull you in. Then, I could be truly happy.

I've watched you with Ass-Lee the Skank, too. The sight of you two holding hands infuriates me. You don't love her. You can't love her. You don't know what you want. Still, it's not nice to taunt me like that. Why do you want to tease me? Have I ever done anything to you but pledge my undying love?

Inbox

From: YourFriend [YourFriend@x_ray-mail.com]
To: NoahW[w.noah@glcuco.com]
Date: September 22, 8:36 PM
Subject: RE: A Proposition

Can you blame me for trying to burn down your parents' house in Rowayton? I had to get your attention somehow! Honestly, I didn't want to hurt anyone, but I AM HURT by your behavior. I don't have much extra pity for anyone else.

I know the cops think the fire was an accident, but it wasn't. I'm taking full credit.

When the gate to your family's estate opened for a delivery, I snuck inside with a five-gallon plastic gasoline can. Yes, I'd been watching and waiting for an opportune time. Your family must shop a lot on Amazon because a delivery truck pulls into your driveway at least three times a week.

Luckily, the garage door was open, so I went inside. After closing the garage door, I poured the gas around the three cars parked there. Your folks own a Mercedes, Jaguar, and a Range Rover. Now, do you believe me when I say I started the fire?

I noticed that the door from the garage into the house was ajar, so I went inside. I looked at all your framed family photos on the mantle above your living room's fireplace.

You and your folks have gone on a lot of expensive-looking trips to different countries. I've never been to Europe. The only trip my mom ever took me on was when we moved from Kansas City to Stamford.

We were running away from my dad because he used to beat the hell out of her. Not exactly a fun vacation, you know?

I will never be a woman like my mother. Taking abuse for all those years… What an idiot. If my dad ever finds us, my angry face will be the last thing he ever sees because I'm going to kill him. I may torture him first, but I haven't figured all that out yet.

Anyhow, I went into your mom's massive kitchen and turned on one of the gas burners in her big Viking range. I felt that turning on all burners might be suspicious, but one burner left on could be deemed an accident. I then returned to the garage, lit a match, and threw it down on the gas. I walked out through the back door, jumped the fence into your neighbor's yard, and hoped for the best.

I didn't know the Jaguar your folks owned was an EV, a Jaguar I-Pace. Were you aware that the model has been recalled because the battery can spontaneously catch fire? It's true. They've stopped making that model. The fact that your parents owned one has turned out to be a stroke of luck for me. From what I gathered from the news, the investigators think the fire started with the I-Pace, and the remnants of gasoline came from your parents' other burned-up cars. All I know is that your house fire made the front page of the Norwalk Daily Voice, but nobody suspected it was arson.

Honestly, I didn't know your housekeeper was upstairs. It's not like the vacuum was running or anything like that. The house was quiet. I'm glad she's still alive.

I can't, however, say the same for Ass-Lee, the student skank. I'm up all night sometimes, imagining all the different ways I can wreck her shit. I'd like to ruin her life just like she's ruining mine.

Too bad I can't get hold of a medieval torture rack.

I feel the change comin', and it's not good, Noah. I'm losing my patience with you. In fact, I've lost it. Do you understand? It's time for you to man up and quit acting like a child.

I have tried and triyed to get in contact with you, and all you do is block me, call the police on me, and now – a restraining odor???? *Order.*

I can't even hink right now, I'm so mad! What is wrong with you? YOU ARE PISSING ME OFF! I CAN"T TAKE IT ANYMORE.

The thought of you with Ass-Lee, the student skank, is two much. I HOPE SHE DIES. And YOU, YOU YOU YOU Y

I will not endure this anymore. I feel brave and daring. I feel emboldened enough to finish what we started that weekend. You can't keep us apart. Not anymore. I feel my blood flow, and my sixth sense tells me it's time to take further action.

I'm coming for you. You have a choice. You either leave with me or deny our love and suffer the consequences. I wll never, ever forget our weekend together. Even if you insist it was just a few miinutes on a Saturday, it was a weekend to me. A precious weekend. Those moments together, the love we have. When will I see you? The answer is SOON, Noah. I'm coming for you. If we can't live on earth together, we'll live together in heaven. Or hell. Your choice.

These emails are submitted as evidence to the Office of the State's Attorney Judicial District of Stamford/Norwalk by Detective Richard Sullivan as part of the case file in the Noah W attempted murder investigation. The suspect, Margaret B, is currently being detained at the Norwalk Jail, Fairfield County.

Can't Smile Without You

Inspired by *Can't Smile Without You* from the album
Even Now (1978)

Caleb Weinhardt

I push my way through the crowd. All these people are here for you, pressed up against each other, snapping flashbulb photographs and smelling like carriage rides and sweat. Don't they know how important I am to you? If they did, surely they would part to let me through.

When I finally squeeze my way to the front, I peer through the smudged glass of the mortuary window. Warmth spreads from my chest all the way to my toes.

Behind the glass, the undertaker in pinstripes shows off his work. Propped up on a slab, there's a boy who had half his face ripped away in a meat-hook incident. Teeth gleam through the torn flesh of his cheek. Beside him, a wrinkled old crone who looks just as much alive as she did a few weeks ago. I make myself wait, linger over these two bodies, before slowly taking you in.

You're dressed in a fine muslin skirt like the day we walked along the river, when I heard that discordant violin in your voice and knew that something was wrong. White gloves still adorn your fingers. Your sunshine hair is chopped abruptly above the shoulders, because it became too tangled as you floated down the Seine. Your eyes are closed, off in a peaceful dream. A smile still lingers on your lips.

There you are.

People have come from all across the country, drawn by those photos of you in the paper. Enamored by your smile, hopelessly under your spell. And yet they don't even know your name.

The undertaker makes his money keeping the viewing window limited to a few hours a day. As he starts to pull the curtains shut, the onlookers protest. They surge forward, and a few even issue threats. They will have to come back tomorrow and pay again.

While they mutter and disperse, someone catches me by the arm. A man with a camera around his neck, big and heavy, and sporting a ruffled, dark mustache. He looks me up and down, takes in the delicate stitching of my dress, and releases me.

"I'm sorry. I mistook you for someone else."

I return to Papa's carriage—he's been waiting for me. Inside, he looks solemn and old. He does not want to look at you the way these people do. He only wants to remember you as you were—bright and vibrant and alive.

He does not look at me or speak as we ride home. He would have spoken to you, I'm sure. You always used to say how he spoke sweetly, and detected your moods, and plied you with candy and gifts when you were sad. He does not do these things for me.

When we get out of the carriage, Papa tips the driver. We begin the long walk up to his estate, his cane tip-tapping against the cobblestone. A man rushes to greet us and walks alongside him, informing him of today's business. Papa nods, not listening, and the man hurries away again.

I offer Papa my hand as we climb the stone steps upward. He looks at it, then finally takes it, begrudgingly. I smile at the way he squeezes it for support, the way his breath falters with each step.

We reach the top of the stairs and he turns to me before going in. His mouth moves searchingly, lips dry. He wets them and tries again.

"We'll go back tomorrow," I say, before he can speak. "Won't we?" I need him to know how much I rely on him and appreciate his generosity. My eyes well with tears, but they don't spill out.

The lines of his face harden. He grips his cane and releases my hand. "I know how important you were to her," he says, dryly. He ambles inside, leaving me on the landing.

* * *

We were girls when we met. We came from the same place—the place with all those rows of rattling white beds and concrete floors and lots of children but no mother and father.

We did have stories we told each other about our parents, though. Estelle said her mother was an angel. It was true. When she slept, she looked as close to angelic as a person can. She thought my parents must have been laborers—my father rowed boats for people along the river, and my mother spun thread. She said she could tell because of my hands, and how I didn't get sick all the time, like she did.

She was so small and pale that I thought she was surely just an angel who had ended up in the wrong place.

Only she could make that place bearable—my constant and closest friend. At night when she was sick and couldn't sleep, I would creep into her bed, and we would play a game only the two of us understood.

First I would frown, and say, "Whose face?"

"Mrs. Hafferty," she would say, and we both giggled.

Then she would pretend to cry, balling her fists at her eyes. This was the girl who kept us all awake, sniffling for her mother through the night.

Then she would smile, showing all her teeth. "Who is this?"

"The Hat Man," I said.

She frowned. "You're supposed to do it too. Like this." She pressed her fingers to the corners of my mouth, drawing them up into a smile. I tried to keep my face stern, but it was impossible. I started to laugh, and the smile she had drawn on my face became real.

And then Mrs. Hafferty would come by and see us giggling when we should have been asleep, and whip the blanket away. She would sigh, one hand on her hip. "In your own beds, girls!"

We called him the Hat Man, the man who came to visit us, because he wore a tall brown top hat, which he always tipped graciously. He had big tufts of hair on his cheeks and wet blue eyes, and his fine clothes drew the attention of every child in the orphanage. They all flocked around him, eyes wide, scratching their bottoms and hoping he might have something for *them* this time.

But he was only there for Estelle. And for me, because I was her friend.

One day, he brought us each gifts wrapped carefully in cloth. Estelle unwrapped hers first—it was an orange! We didn't get fresh fruit often, and I saw how happy this made her. I smiled along.

In my pouch: two small plums.

"Because you're sweet as a plumb!" Estelle told me, half-convincing.

She nudged me, so I smiled up at the Hat Man and told him, "Thank you very much, sir."

By that summer, our legs got long and we got restless. Estelle liked to watch the boys play in the chain-fenced yard through the window. One of them, a boy with freckles and dirty socks, would look up at her and grin a toothy grin. She would rest her chin on her hands and say, "I think I'll marry him one day."

"I'll never get married," I told her.

"Don't say that! One day we'll both be married, and we'll live down the street from each other and spend every day together." She was smiling, so I smiled too. I liked this idea, aside from the marriage part.

All that time she spent watching the boys, I spent watching her. The way she twisted her hair or bit her lower lip when she was concentrating. I caught myself doing these things too, imagining what it would feel like to be pretty, for someone to see me and think, *look how lost in thought she is. I wonder what she's thinking about? It must be something very important.*

The Hat Man continued to come. Estelle gushed about him when he was gone, waiting anxiously for his visits. "What do you think he'll bring me next?" She asked. "What do you think his wife is like? I bet she's beautiful, and kind." And, "Do you think he has any children?"

"Of course not," I said. "Why do you think he comes here?"

As it turned out, the Hat Man had two older sons, but no daughters, and his wife had died many years ago. It made him sad, since he had always wanted a girl. Eventually, he chose Estelle to fill that hole in his life.

It didn't come as a surprise to me—he had always favored her. But I also expected her to demand I go with her. We were sisters, more than sisters, though not by blood. If he wanted her, I was just a part of the arrangement. I would always be second-best, never the object of his affections, but he would humor me. For Estelle.

But that was not how it happened. It all happened in secret, and she didn't tell me a thing until she was already packing her clothes.

"Are you going away?"

She smoothed her clothes down in a suitcase that didn't belong to her. She was wearing a new pink ribbon in her hair. "Yes," she said at last. She smiled at me softly, and then sat down on my bed. She took my hand. "You can come visit me anytime you like."

A knot was rising in my throat. "Mrs. Hafferty would never let me."

"Then we'll come get you!" She said. "Papa says we'll go away to the ocean sometimes, and you can come with us. Did you know you can see the other side of the world across the ocean?"

I took my hand away. She looked hurt, and touched my cheek. "Don't be sad, Lorraine."

I turned away and rose from the bed. "I'm not."

She packed the rest of her things while I watched from the windowsill. Then she hugged me goodbye and wiped a tear from her cheek. I thought I should cry, but didn't. She smiled, and I smiled back.

I wouldn't even miss her, I told myself. Not after she'd abandoned me so easily. And if she called after me again, I would refuse to see her.

I stewed in this righteous anger for weeks. When months passed, it was replaced by a quiet hollow in my stomach. Mrs. Hafferty said I looked ill, but didn't call for a doctor. These things pass, she said, even though she had coddled Estelle at the slightest hint of illness. As long as she was well and smiling, Mrs. Hafferty had nothing to fear from the inspectors who looked for signs of bruises and neglect. Their eyes passed over me with little concern.

Still, I kept waiting for her to sneak into my bed after the other children were asleep—to grab me by the toe and surprise me, to show me another face I had to guess at. Most importantly, that face would be her own.

* * *

When I was too old to stay there any longer, Mrs. Hafferty told me I could look for work as a maid. If I could learn to be polite and keep myself clean, that is. She sent me off and washed her hands of me.

And then I was outside in the rush of air and people, with so many strong smells—horse manure and urine, coal fire, sweat and hay—everyone on their way to someplace, and me, lost in all of it.

First I went to an inn and asked for something to eat.

"Can you pay?" The innkeeper raked her fingers through frazzled, graying hair.

I felt around in my pockets, knowing they would be empty. "I can work."

"Payin' customers only. Take yourself elsewhere." And she swept me out into the street.

I slept in a stable that first night, straw pricking me through my clothes, and stayed until the innkeeper threw me out.

I wandered for some time. I kept asking: for work, for a bed, for half a franc, but the longer I went, the more matted my hair became, and the dirtier my fingernails, and I knew that no one would invite me into a respectable home. I began to see other shadow people who had learned to make themselves small, invisible, and in this way sometimes inspired pity. More often, though, scorn and brutality. I watched as a woman was beaten when she reached out to touch a gentleman's coat, and learned quickly not to touch. I saw a boy catch ill and turn a sickly blue from sleeping on the street, so I collected papers and empty sacks to sleep on. I took the shape of a shadow too.

I thought of her sometimes. Where she must be now, attending fancy balls with her Papa, eating cakes and drinking coffee, no trace of her previous life left to stink on her. I thought she might look very beautiful now. Sometimes my memory of her was clear, and her voice sounded as if it was there in my ear, whispering under the blankets. Other times I would try to remember her and find nothing at all.

I took up begging at one market in particular, where the merchants sometimes gave away scraps they couldn't sell, and the customers were sometimes generous. I looked for Estelle in the faces of the women who passed through, with their large bustles and powdered cheeks. She would not be so garish, I thought. Or so old. Their gloved fingers moved brutishly as they picked their vegetables and counted their coins. She would be much more delicate, thoughtful. She would smile at the merchant, and he would be unable to stop himself from smiling too, not quite knowing why.

While I pictured this, I smiled dumbly to myself. I hardly even realized it until another shadow woman caught my eye with that ever-questioning glare. *We do not smile. We do not speak. We take what we are given.*

So I stopped looking for her.

* * *

I was in my usual spot, tucked against a sweating wall of stone along the alley where all the customers passed on their way home, when it happened.

Though it was really only the children who garnered any sort of compassion, I kept my hands outstretched as long as my arms would hold them. What I hoped for, more, was those end-of-day scraps that would sustain me another night. Most of the time, I didn't even bother to look at the passersby. But this day, I felt something incredible: the cool touch of a coin in my hands.

They dipped under the unexpected weight, then closed around it. I looked up at the gloved hand that had deposited it, and up the arm to wide blue eyes.

Her hat was tied under her chin with a silk scarf, and her hair was rolled into tight blonde curls. The look on her face was one of surprise, then recognition.

I was suddenly aware of the way I looked and smelled, and couldn't stand for her to see me that way. Perhaps she hadn't placed me yet in her memory, and would still think of me as the little girl at the orphanage who was her friend, who made her laugh. So I ran and didn't look back, and didn't listen to hear if she called after me.

* * *

The encounter had filled me with a dizzying excitement. She was here, within reach! Perhaps we had lived within feet of each other for years without knowing it. Suddenly I wondered if she had gone back to the orphanage to ask for me, to see if Mrs. Hafferty knew where I had gone. Perhaps she had been sad not to find me, even after all these years of absence. Perhaps she had been looking too, searching for me when her mind was idle, imagining what life I had made for myself.

With this new possibility in mind, I was determined to find her again.

I washed myself in the river, and did the best I could to comb the tangles from my hair with my fingers. I didn't even think of the wayward glances of shadow women. For my clothes, there was little to be done. I stole two small loaves of bread while a merchant was busy disciplining a clumsy child, and even managed to find a stray beet that had rolled away from a vegetable cart. I used this to put some redness in my cheeks.

And then I waited, every day for a week, behind the wall at the end of the alley so that I could see her before she saw me. I kept catching glimpses of a white glove, a lock of blonde hair, and felt my heart beat fast, only for the woman to turn and be someone else.

At last, she came. She was with her Papa, who looked much the same but with a little more gray. I could see her fully this time—she had grown tall and pleasantly thin, and her face was clear and gentle as she spoke to the merchants, and turned to laugh to Papa. As they were leaving, arm-in-arm, I stepped out into the crowd and wove my way toward her.

This time, she recognized me with a look of disbelief. "Lorraine! Is that you?" She left Papa behind and pushed toward me, taking hold of my arm. "I thought I saw you, but then you ran away—!"

"I was just buying bread." I forced one of the loaves into her hands, keeping the smaller of the two for myself. "Here, please have some."

"Oh, no. I couldn't, really!"

"I insist." I smiled. Slowly, she smiled back.

Papa caught up to her. "Papa, do you remember Lorraine?"

He looked over me with the hardened gaze he'd always reserved for me. "Of course." He smiled at Estelle. "How could I forget your little friend?"

"Oh, we must show her our home." She hung on him, pleading. "Can't we?"

Although it looked like it pained him slightly, he agreed.

We rode back in a carriage—Papa even helped me up the steps. I tried not to stare too long at the polished black wood or the patterned seat covers as we rocked over the cobblestone street. I clutched my bread tightly. Although I was anxious to eat, I couldn't think of doing it in front of her.

She asked me things about my life. "Do you live nearby?"

"Yes, I have a room with a family here."

"How wonderful you've found a family, Lorraine!"

"Well, I clean for them."

"Oh," she said. After a moment, she smiled again and squeezed my hand. "I really am so glad to see you. I've been so lonely without a friend, just me and Papa." She laughed affectionately, and I laughed too. It was hard not to feel the spread of her warmth, thawing me from a deep freeze. I was beginning to feel like myself again.

The house was like nothing I could have imagined. A palace of white and vaulted ceilings and endless staircases, and a menagerie of staff that spun and cooked and cleaned at all hours of the day. Estelle showed me to her room, which had a grand window overlooking the rose garden below.

"What part of the city do you stay in?"

"By Saint-Eustache," I told her.

"Well, you could stay here if you wanted. I would have to ask Papa, of course, but I'm sure he'd say yes."

My cheeks rushed with heat, but I tried to keep my voice steady. "Really?"

"Only if you want to. I'm sure your room is nice enough." She bunched her shoulders up to her ears, her mouth twisting into a half-frown.

"Yes," I said, breathlessly, afraid she would change her mind. "Yes, I would love to stay."

* * *

Those first few weeks were perfect—almost like old times. I bathed in scented water and was attended by two ladies maids, who dressed me in fine clothes. Papa had a dress made up for me. Estelle and I took together walks around the park, counting ducks along the river.

But I found that Estelle had not been entirely honest with me about it being just her and Papa at the house. They lived alone, but she had a persistent visitor. His name was François, and he came to the door every week with flowers. He had a permanently scrunched-up nose, and a smile like the sun was in his eyes, and he was trying to blink away its glare with unusually heavy lashes.

At first I thought nothing of him. She was far too smart to fall for his petty attentions; he wanted nothing good with her. Couldn't she see that? He would only use her up and throw her away. She might smile and bat her eyes, but it was always a ploy, wasn't it?

Inconceivably, Estelle found him charming. She hid it well, feigning disinterest. But I always saw that glow in her once he left. Then, only then, would she take my hand tightly and hold it to her chest.

"Did you see the way he looked at me?" She said. "I think he's going to speak to Papa soon."

"What for?" I asked, not wanting to hear the answer.

"Don't be silly, Lorraine. Don't you know how these things work?"

When I didn't reply, she sighed, longingly. "I want you to be there." She beamed. "On my wedding day."

That's when I knew she would be taken away from me again, right after I'd found her. When she married him, it would end things forever between us. She couldn't take me with her. And I did not want to follow at her heels, watching her with *him*.

He would sleep in her bed. All her smiles for him alone. And eventually, after a time—many years, if I was lucky—she would forget she had ever known me.

I tried to remind her of how things were before, but she went silent when I spoke of the orphanage. She couldn't see what it meant to me. I knew I would have to show her.

One night, I pushed open her door and stepped into the darkness. I told her I couldn't get to sleep. She sat up in bed, eyes bleary, and beckoned me close.

I got under the covers, feeling her warmth. We looked at each other, blinking. I touched her cheek, gently. I felt the corners of her mouth and tried to push them into a smile, but she slapped my hands away.

"What are you doing?" she asked, staring at me with disgust.

"It's the game we used to play. Don't you remember?"

"We're not children anymore."

She let me sleep in her bed, but it was as if I was entirely alone. She turned onto her side so that her back faced me, cold and stoic. I wanted so badly to reach out and touch her, but her body stiffened at my approach.

I fell asleep counting her breaths.

* * *

Estelle convinced Papa we could go to the market on our own. She begged him, saying that some things a woman needed were not for him to see.

It was perfume she wanted, something to dab behind her ears for François to notice the next time he came by. She would turn him away, as usual, but the scent of desire on her would leave him no choice but to ask Papa for her hand. At least, that was her plan.

The perfumer was on a bustling street with all the best wig-makers and doctors, and came to greet us right away. He was a short man, and he fawned over Estelle immediately, knowing it was her the perfume would adorn. Somehow, even in fine clothes, people could see that I was not quite like her.

We followed him to the back of the shop, where we tried on various scents. I found the man peevish and incessant, and no help at all, and eventually told him we could look for ourselves. I used my best "gentle lady" voice, which made Estelle laugh.

I flushed. "What is it?"

"You shouldn't talk like that. It sounds unnatural on you."

I tried not to let the sting linger too long. "Unnatural? And what do you call this?" I took a vial of perfume from the shelf. "Dousing yourself in deer… excrement?"

The perfumer eyed me warily. "It's called *Tawny Woodpecker.*"

I flashed Estelle a look, happy to be in on a joke together. "Whatever that smells like."

She giggled.

We sampled various scents, but I thought none of them were better than the way she smelled already—just warm and peachy, like fresh fruit. Eventually she chose something called "Rosebud Daffodil." It was far too pungent for me.

It was almost dark when we left, only a few lingering shadows in the street. We walked back along the river, a skip in her step and a drag in mine. The closer we got to home, the sooner this day would end, and she would turn all her attentions on François again.

"Don't you think you're rushing things?" I asked her, trying to get the words out before my confidence vanished again.

She looked aghast. "How can you say that, Lorraine? Aren't you happy for me?"

"Of course I want *you* to be happy. But is this really what you want?"

Estelle stopped walking. She toyed with a ring on her finger—a gift from Papa, right after he adopted her. "You would understand if you'd ever been in love."

I didn't know how to explain, how to tell her. Her mouth was turned into a pitiful frown, the corners of her lips tensed. I watched her blue eyes move over me. Always discerning, but never *seeing*. All I wanted was for her to smile and tell me how silly she'd been, how she couldn't believe she had actually considered *marrying* François. How she couldn't risk losing me.

So I reached for her hand, hoping my touch might speak to her in a way my words could not, but as I did, I realized I was also pushing her. Her eyes darted wide as her heels tipped over the stone. Her arms reached for me.

There was a loud crash when she hit the water, churning up bubbles. She did not surface for a while, and then came up gasping. Her dress billowed around her, blonde curls plastered to her face.

"Lorraine, help me!"

I watched, my face turning to her face—that expression of disbelief. *How could you? How could you? How could you do this to me?*

I watched her sink.

I stood there a long time, waiting to see her come up again, or for someone to come along and see the vile thing I had done. Neither came.

* * *

It took you three weeks to be found. In that time, you had traveled seven miles downriver, and became entangled in one of the locks near a park where families take their children on sunny days. It was one of these families that saw you floating—not face-down, like you might imagine a corpse to float, but on your back, as if taking in the rays of sun through parted clouds. On your face, an expression of serenity. You had just closed your eyes to dream, to drift along the current, the mucky water made pure by your presence.

In those three weeks, I was wracked by anxiety. Would you ever surface again? Would suspicions turn on me, if you did? But I felt such relief to see your face again in that display window that all my fears melted away. I was so glad to see your smile.

They ruled it a suicide, and Papa was too ashamed to claim your body. He said you wouldn't go to Heaven for what you'd done, and I think he felt you had wronged him deeply by taking yourself away from him.

I loosed tears easily this time, as I thought I should. Papa let me sleep in your bed, wear your clothes, soak in the smell of you. I was in mourning, after all.

François took his leave of us, dejected, after offering all the scraps of comfort he could muster. Really, it was not me or Papa he cared for, and so he moved on to find some other pretty girl whose smile would never be quite like yours.

And I stayed here.

I go to visit you every day, until one day they decide you are too precious to display for the common folk on the street. Someone casts your face in plaster to immortalize your beauty—hangs it on a wall. I would like to find the art seller making a fortune off of these casts, but Papa would never allow it.

Still, I have the photographs in the paper. It gives me comfort to know you rest peacefully, that you will never leave me behind again. The last name on your lips was mine.

On every occasion I can, when I have some privacy, I look at the paper with your photograph on the front page. I study your face, your smile. I touch the corners of my mouth and move them into the same expression. I close my eyes and imagine myself floating on the water.

Ready to Take a Chance Again

Inspired by *Ready to Take a Chance Again* from the album
Foul Play: Original Motion Picture Soundtrack (1978)

Kurtis Rupé

The scent of disinfectant and the hum from overhead tube lighting hung in the air as Geri entered Armand's hospital room. He reclined against the raised back of the hospital bed, his face bruised and swollen, his arm in a sling, encased like a mummy in a wrap of medical tape wound around his chest. The attack had left its mark on him.

"Geri," he rasped.

"Armand," she whispered, pulling a chair close to the bed. "How are you feeling?"

"Pain meds work, but everything is hazy," he said with a weak smile. "Doctor thinks I'll heal in a few weeks." Then he paused. "At least physically."

Speaking quietly together, Geri mentioned she would see Vance's press conference in front of Marina Vista City Hall before she returned to the office.

Armand listened, his grip tightening on the bed sheet.

"He's a snake," Armand croaked. "Don't let him fool you."

"I won't," Geri whispered, her voice quivering. "I'm going to get to the bottom of this, Armand. I promise."

But even as the words left her lips, she felt doubt creeping into her heart. The forces that sought to silence Armand and the community of Pride Point, aligning to erase their very existence, appeared potent and merciless.

* * *

It had only been three days earlier that Geri trudged the four blocks back to the Palm Terrace apartments, her shoulder-length dark hair pulled back in a practical ponytail, her small blue backpack slung over one shoulder, another dreary day the same as every day for the past month. The "June gloom" is what locals called it in Marina Vista, California, with overcast grey skies and cooler temperatures. It felt like being in purgatory, as monotonous and disappointing as everything these days and not at all the year-round sun and fun she expected from California when she moved here after college, with Marisol.

Today included one more letdown. Geri had screwed up her courage to go and see Lottie, owner-manager of The Salty Siren, about getting on the list for open mic night. It had taken all her courage, knowing it meant committing to performing for an audience. But the tough-looking and intimidating Lottie, six-foot-two, with a crewcut and a muscle shirt that did not hide her ink or nipple piercings, delivered the news to Geri softly, with a catch in her voice: "Sorry, Kid. We're closing for good by next Monday, we finally had to sell out to Vance. Couldn't keep up with the health and safety code violations."

"What do you mean?" Geri asked, "I don't understand."

"The constant hassle for the past month, one thing after another," she explained. "After we close at night, someone destroys the handrails to the entrance, and the next day, a cop shows up and issues a ticket with a hefty fine. Before I can even get it replaced, something happens again the next night. In the wee hours, someone takes a sledgehammer to a water pipe, cop shows up in the morning, issues another violation for water running on the sidewalk." Then she turned away, brushing a tear from her eyes. "I'm being muscled out, and I can't do it anymore."

* * *

When Geri turned the key to the deadbolt, she unconsciously checked her phone. There were no messages, only Marisol's photo on the cover screen, caught mid-laugh, twisting away from the camera. Inside the apartment, it felt so empty that she imagined an echo as she closed the door and dropped her backpack on the coffee table.

The turntable sat on top of a plastic crate in the corner with about a dozen vinyl LPs stacked near it. These were the Barry Manilow records of Geri's that Marisol didn't take. "I never liked Barry Manilow as much as you," Marisol said when they ended it last month, somewhere in between, "We're not the same people," "I'm just not in love with you," and "I think we both deserve to be happy."

There were blank spaces, too, where Marisol had taken her paintings from the wall. She had left the unframed painting that hung near the door, though, the one she made for Geri shortly after they became a couple. It was an idealized image of a sunset, orange above the blue ocean, and a warm sandy beach with the superimposed text of a Barry Manilow quote: "You've got to save yourself. Nobody is going to give you anything. You've got to go out and fight for it. Nobody knows what you want except you, and nobody will be as sorry as you if you don't get it. So don't give up on your dreams." Geri saw this every day upon entering and leaving the apartment but lately hardly noticed it.

They had moved to Pride Point, a gay-friendly neighborhood just three blocks from the pier and the beach, close to the exit for Marina Vista's business district, because it offered something they couldn't find in either the university town they had left or the stultifying place where Geri grew up. At first, it was intimidating. The people she met were so vibrant, wild, alive, and free, unlike how she perceived herself. Still, she sensed she could be whoever she wanted to be here, if she could figure out who that was.

She and Marisol used to hold hands when they walked to The Salty Siren for beers and fish tacos, which they couldn't do before they came here. On the weekends, they perused the used books and LPs at Rainbow Sands Book & Vinyl Emporium, listening as the owner, Armand Derian, a tall, thin man in his fifties with tortoiseshell glasses perched on his nose, discoursed with patrons about everything from jazz to mystery novels to local politics. The fact that he was a candidate for city council in the upcoming election elevated him in Geri's mind.

Geri thought Armand would be a fine representative for Pride Point in city affairs.

Donovan Vance was also a candidate for city council in the upcoming election and a white guy in his fifties. He carried a paunch in his midsection, wore expensive suits with gold cufflinks, grew a grey-haired ponytail behind his balding scalp in front, and had two pale blue eyes dotting his jowly face. On local news broadcasts, Geri had seen him making reprehensible speeches about her LGBTQ+ neighborhood, calling its inhabitants vermin and pedophiles. He operated a janitorial services company and dabbled in local real estate. Still, in Geri's opinion, he was flashy-rich, not classy-rich, with the chunky gold ring that he waved around when he talked. He planned to secure a seat on the city council by stirring up the bigots and promising a "family-friendly" city, which would help him to push for the redevelopment of Pride Point and further enrich himself.

* * *

Geri congratulated herself on arriving at work on time, a feat she had inconsistently achieved in recent weeks. She heard voices drifting from the break room before Olivia and Blake stopped by her desk with their morning coffee.

"You hear about Rainbow Sands?" Blake asked.

Her head shot up. Not only did she like to visit that book and record store, but Armand Derian was a client, and she managed his insurance program.

"Vandalized," Olivia said, her voice somber. "In the middle of the night. Broken window, spray-painted graffiti…" Her voice trailed off, her face an expression of disgust and anger.

"Haters and bigots," Blake spat, brow furrowed. "What is wrong with people? Why can't they just leave us alone?"

Their shared outrage drew a sympathetic smile from Geri, who felt a surge of protectiveness toward Armand and his store. This wasn't the first time in recent weeks that such things had happened in Pride Point. More intolerant agitators had come around, emboldened by a change in the larger political climate.

Before they could discuss it further, the front door swung open, and Armand himself hurried in, a pained expression on his face.

"Mr. Derian," Geri said quickly, standing to meet him. "I just heard what happened. I am so sorry it happened to you. Please sit down, and I will get this claim paid quickly."

Armand described the shattered window and hateful message scrawled on the storefront. From his phone, he showed Geri a video clip captured by security cameras, and then he emailed it to her for the claim file. The video revealed a masked figure in a hoodie taking a sledgehammer to the window, spray-painting malicious words, climbing into a white Ford Transit van, and speeding away.

"A policeman came by this morning," Armand said. "Officer Russell Cox took my information, told me he'd review the video footage and investigate but, frankly, not to expect they'd catch the guy. He said he would send a police report for insurance purposes shortly. I gave him your contact information."

He mentioned a few other incidents in the past weeks—protests on the sidewalk in front of the store against a children's story time event and a disrupted author signing for a YA book with LGBTQ+ themes.

Dread pooled in Geri's stomach. This wasn't about a broken window but a community under siege. Memories of struggles and anxieties back in her old hometown resurfaced. But having spent a few minutes with Armand, hearing the strength in his voice despite the ugliness directed at him had sparked within her a feeling she hadn't felt in a long time – a flame of determination pushing against the tide of shadows.

Armand sighed, his shoulders sagging slightly. "It's an attack on what we stand for, Geri. Inclusion, acceptance, equality... things some folks seem to find threatening." His words hung there as Geri met his gaze. How could she sit around and watch as bigots and criminals unjustly destroyed her community?

⋆ ⋆ ⋆

After he had gone, she looked at Blake and Olivia to see their reaction.

"This isn't about an insurance claim. It's about Pride Point and pushing people out by making them afraid," she said, the tone of her voice dropping. "But what can we do?"

Geri suspected the cause behind the damage was Donovan Vance, with his hateful rhetoric and redevelopment plans threatening the end of Pride Point. She mulled her reasoning, connecting the dots from Vance's agenda to the pattern of escalating harassment in the neighborhood.

The three formulated a plan for her to investigate as part of her claim administration. She could begin by talking further with Armand and anyone else who may know something about the vandalism at Rainbow Sands, reviewing the security footage and loss information.

"There's someone else you should talk to," Blake suggested. "Andrea MacDonald. She manages Surfside Grind, across the street from Armand's place. She may have some intel, and she's not afraid to say what's on her mind."

Geri's eyes lit up. She knew Andrea as the enchanting barista with whom she made small talk waiting for her chai soy latte. Geri felt the slightest twinge of guilt as she went back to her desk. Marisol had not crossed her mind all morning.

* * *

Usually, Geri could see the pier from the entrance to Surfside Grind, but now, the coastal blanket of fog obscured it. As she opened the door, a warm breath of air swirling in earthy notes of coffee beans and the sweet, spicy bouquet of cinnamon, cardamom, and cloves enveloped her. Behind the counter stood a brown-skinned woman about her age, a short afro above a warm smile and brown eyes. "Hey," Geri greeted, the usual awkwardness she felt around people absent. "That Barry Manilow song playing… unexpected choice."

Andrea chuckled, one gold hoop earring flashing near her throat. "Unexpected? Maybe. But sometimes, the classics need a little reinterpretation." She gestured to the espresso machine behind her. "Like a good cup of coffee."

A conversation blossomed, fueled by a shared love of music and a discovery—Andrea herself was a musician, a keyboardist, and a singer. They delved into their experiences, the challenges they faced, and the dreams they held close. Emboldened by Andrea's infectious energy and playful spirit, Geri confessed her own musical aspirations—songwriting and rearranging Barry Manilow tunes into soulful jazz fusions.

Andrea's eyes widened with genuine enthusiasm. "You play and write songs? Geri, that's amazing! We're having our first open mic night here next month. You should totally sign up!"

Nervous excitement washed over Geri. Performing in front of strangers was terrifying, but the idea of taking a risk resonated. This open mic night may be an opportunity to step outside her comfort zone.

"Sometimes, Geri," Andrea said, her voice rich and robust as her coffee, her hand sliding across the tabletop, "the best things in life happen when you take a chance."

* * *

Geri hardly noticed the June gloom when she left Surfside Grinds and crossed the street to Rainbow Sands Books & Vinyl Emporium. The newly boarded-up window provoked a fresh gust of anger that she pushed away as she entered the familiar scent of books and possibility. Armand Derian sat behind the counter, his face a picture of worry.

"Hello again, Mr. Derian," Geri began, her voice firm but sympathetic. "I'm doing more investigation, going up and down the street asking if anyone knows anything that might bring these thugs to justice. May I start with you? Is there any more information about last night that we didn't already cover this morning?"

Armand sighed, pushing his glasses up on his nose. "More than information, my dear," he said. "It's the relentless harassment. Donovan Vance has been pressuring me to sell him my building for months. He offers a pittance, nowhere near market value, even if I did want to sell."

She frowned. Armand's revelation clarified Vance's motive.

Acquiring the building at a cut-rate price would be a coup for his redevelopment plan profit. "Does Mr. Vance say why he's so insistent on buying?" she inquired.

"He spouts the usual nonsense about progress and modernization," Armand scoffed. "He wants to tear down all of Pride Point and replace it with overpriced condos and shopping. This bookstore, my home – it all stands in his way."

* * *

Stepping back into muted afternoon daylight, she decided to canvass nearby businesses, hoping someone might have witnessed something.

It was mostly unproductive. Nobody was around at that time of night, but she left her business card at a few retail stores that had cameras facing the street or in the direction of Rainbow Sands. She asked them to pull their videos and email them to her. She noted that they said no one besides her had yet come around to investigate, certainly no one from the police.

She was about to head back to the office when she spotted Finn Taylor, a laid-back surfer with sun-bleached hair and a perpetual chill vibe. Geri remembered him as a budtender from occasional visits to her local cannabis dispensary. He had a laid-back demeanor, but his eyes held a quiet intelligence.

"Hey, Finn," Geri greeted him. "I'm looking into the vandalism at Rainbow Sands. Did you happen to see anything the other night?"

Finn squinted thoughtfully, running a hand through his hair. "Totally, dude," he drawled. "I was coming back from a night surfing sesh, carrying my board on the sidewalk, and this white van comes hauling ass from in front of the bookstore. That's pretty sus, right?"

A jolt of excitement shot through Geri. "Did you catch anything else? Maybe a license plate or something about the van?"

Finn grinned. "I couldn't get the full license plate—it went down real quick, and it was dark—but I saw the last 3 digits: 007, like a Bond movie with Daniel Craig." He paused a moment, then continued. "Oh, and check this out: there was a 'How's My Driving?' sticker slapped on the back door, blue with yellow letters." Then he snorted back a chuckle. "Isn't that a joke? That guy's driving was, like, for shit."

With a partial license plate number and the bumper sticker, she had a piece of added information, a new detail to the white van description, and, potentially, a means to identify the culprit. She thanked Finn, a renewed sense of purpose fueling her steps as she returned to the office.

* * *

The insurance office buzzed with a familiar energy as Geri came through the door, her steps infused with purpose. She pulled up Donovan Vance's client file in her computer, uncovering a connection: Vance's janitorial business used white Ford Transit vans. Geri scrolled and clicked into a subfile for a list with their vehicle information and license plate data. And she found it there: eight white Ford Transit panel vans with customized sequential license plates that read VJS 001 through VJS 008.

"Score!" Geri exclaimed, a triumphant grin spreading across her face.

* * *

There was still no copy of Officer Cox's police report—she thought she'd have it by now. She sent a business-like email requesting it from Cox and cc'ing her client, Armand Derian.

She did find an email from Wavecrest Jewels & Gifts, a retail jewelry store near Rainbow Sands, on the other side of the street.

The email attachment was a security video. Their camera angle picked up the street and sidewalk through the display case window, and, at 3:34 a.m. last night, a white Ford Transit van zipped past and slowed to turn left onto a side street. Geri replayed it, advancing the video slowly with her mouse. Right there, a little fuzzy but quite readable on the rear bumper, was license plate number VJS 007 and a 'How's My Driving?' sticker on the rear door, blue with yellow letters.

* * *

She didn't stop there. A flurry of online searches led her down a rabbit hole of local forums and social media groups. She typed in keywords – "white van," "How's My Driving?" sticker, "Pride Point" – hoping for a shred of additional information.

She found a blurry photo on a neighborhood watch page depicting a white van parked outside an office building, a familiar sticker gleaming on the rear window. Checking the address online against city tax records confirmed that it was owned by Vance Janitorial Services, Inc. This could be a useful item in her quest!

But the discovery brought questions. How could Vance, with a modest local janitorial service company, afford such a prominent office location in an expensive area? Such businesses would usually have been in a warehouse or industrial building, one with secure parking for its small fleet of vans. Instead, Vance owned a glass-and-steel office building in Sterling Plaza, the best office complex in the Elite Harbor district of Marina Vista, with upscale businesses, luxury amenities, and high property values. Something was wrong with this picture. Was Vance getting revenue from an illicit source? Could there be something more sinister than harassment and vandalism going on? She might be jumping to conclusions, but it felt important to consider.

On a whim, Geri typed Officer Russell Cox onto her screen. A deep dive into online forums uncovered profiles under his name spewing hateful rhetoric and aligning with well-known extremist groups. Cox's online presence exposed a potential motive for ignoring the harassment – or even participating in it – prejudice against those who, like Armand Derian, embraced diversity. Maybe he was on Vance's payroll or under his thumb somehow? This thought chilled her.

* * *

Geri sat cross-legged on the floor of her dimly lit apartment, her fingers dancing over the guitar strings, coaxing melodic notes out as she leaned forward, cradling it against her torso with effortless elegance. She felt the quiet hum of satisfaction within her. The day's progress fueled a sense of optimism. The connection with Finn and the incriminating videos of the van felt like a step in the right direction. She felt a smile grow as the melody of "Ready to Take a Chance Again" began taking shape.

Suddenly, the ringtone on her phone shattered the tranquility. Unknown Caller. A knot formed in Geri's stomach as she picked it up. A raspy, distorted voice filled her ear.

"You're asking too many questions, you uppity bitch," the creepy voice snarled. "Back the fuck off, or you'll be sorry."

Panic prickled Geri's skin, but a glint of defiance sparked in her eyes. Before she could retort, the line went dead, and all she heard was her own heart hammering in her chest.

* * *

The ocean air cast a damp chill that clung to Geri and Andrea as they rounded the corner. A misty fog blanketed the street and sidewalk, obscuring the familiar face of Rainbow Sands Books. Still, the red pulsating lightbar of a paramedic vehicle in front stole Geri's breath.

A lone figure hunched over a motionless body on the steps. A shiver ran through Andrea's hand as it clutched Geri's. "What's happening?" Andrea's voice, barely above a whisper, said as a small crowd gathered at the periphery.

Geri forced herself forward, her legs shaky despite the firm grip of Andrea's hand. As they drew closer, the frantic precision of the paramedic's gloved hand on a prone figure became clear. It was Armand's body lying limp and motionless.

A woman in a blue paramedic's uniform looked up. "Just arrived on the scene," she explained. "Found him like this. We're stabilizing him now, but…" she trailed off as she returned her attention to Armand's face.

"Nine-fifteen. That's when I called nine-one-one," another voice said, an elderly woman with a wool blanket draped over her shoulders. "There was a commotion, a guy shouting 'help,' then nothing." Barely fifteen minutes ago, Armand had likely been putting the finishing touches on closing up shop.

"They hurt Armand," she whispered to Andrea, voice trembling. Andrea's eyes widened, and she pulled Geri into a comforting hug, a brief refuge from the tempest brewing inside Geri. "We need to do something, Andrea. We must expose them before it's too late."

* * *

After visiting Armand in the hospital, Geri went to the press conference. The grey sky cast subdued light on the lawn under the grove of eucalyptus trees in front of Marina Vista City Hall, their silvery leaves rustling in the breeze, their scent mingling with the earthy odor of damp grass. In a tailored pinstripe suit, Donovan Vance stood on a stage in front of a slide projection of his image, smirking to the camera with Old Glory unfurled, giving his viewers the "thumbs up" gesture.

Folding chairs held the hindquarters of a hundred or so Marina Vista residents, many older folks in casual clothes and scowling faces, and about a dozen men in their twenties and thirties in camouflage clothing with tactical gear. Geri knew they weren't real military by their lack of deportment and scruffy beard growth, and she didn't like the open-carry pistols strapped onto their hips or thighs. A few journalists stood at the front, maintaining neutral expressions.

Vance's voice boomed through the speakers, promising a return to a bygone era of prosperity and family values. Perched on a seat in the back, Geri watched and listened with a vague and growing sense of unease.

"Marina Vista deserves better!" he declared, gesturing towards a poster of an artist's rendering of a future Pride Point – a sanitized row of modern retail spaces devoid of rainbow flags and nonwhite shoppers that boasted new franchise restaurants and boutiques, with an astonishing quantity of American Flags displayed. "Pride Point has become a refuge for...undesirables," he continued, "driving away decent families and businesses."

A murmur of agreement rippled through the crowd, people nodding enthusiastically as Vance's veiled rhetoric struck a chord with their discontent.

He discussed his redevelopment plan, a return to the "glory days" of an idealized past. Geri saw through the façade. This wasn't about progress for the city. It was about wiping away the diverse, inclusive spirit that gave Pride Point its very name. Applause erupted as Vance finished his speech, and Geri felt an icy dread settle in her stomach.

* * *

Geri gripped the steering wheel of the car with the familiar agency logo emblazoned on the side when a piercing siren suddenly squawked behind her. She glanced in the mirror to see a squad car's flashing blue and red lights. "Shit, shit, shit," she muttered and pulled to the curb, turned the engine off. "What did I do?"

Officer Russell Cox approached, his eyes hidden behind mirrored aviators. "Ms. Montesquieu," he said in a clipped tone. "Didn't come to a full and complete stop when you made that right turn, did you?"

Geri frowned. She distinctly remembered the light had been yellow, turning red well after she made her turn into Baldwin Avenue. "I thought it was yellow," she stammered.

"Thought?" Cox scoffed, barely concealing a sneer. "This isn't a game, ma'am. Rolling stops are a violation of the vehicle code, and they cause serious accidents."

Geri felt a spark of irritation. "But it was…" she began, then stopped herself. It would do her no good to argue. "Officer, is there something else going on here?"

Cox leaned closer, the volume of his voice dropping. "You've been asking a lot of questions, Ms. Montesquieu. Digging around where you shouldn't." He paused there, letting the implicit threat seep in. "Maybe you should focus on your day job, selling insurance or whatever. Leave police work to the professionals."

Geri's blood ran cold. This was about Armand. The realization slammed into her like a fist. "You have no right to—" she began, but Cox cut her off.

"Just a friendly warning," he said, dripping with condescension. "Make sure you stop completely next time." He sauntered back to his patrol car, leaving Geri fuming behind the wheel.

* * *

Geri slumped in her desk chair, staring at the glowing screen. Taking a break, she looked outside at the grey, muted street and was disheartened by an increasing number of shops sporting "For Sale" signs, imagining conversations laced with fear and resignation. A screen in the break roomg blared Vance's campaign ad for the city council election, his voice promising to "Make Marina Vista great again" as images rolled by of shiny new enclaves for the wealthy and sanitized crime-free streets. Great for whom, she thought? It was not great for the LGBTQ+ community that breathed life into the neighborhood.

* * *

Geri texted Andrea, and not long after, she found herself enveloped in the warmth of the Surfside Grind.

Andrea greeted her with a worried glance, sensing the turmoil behind Geri's forced smile. "I'm going on a break," she said over her shoulder to Terrance, one of her excellent employees, as she and Geri left to walk the pier. Breezy gusts of salt air pulled at their hair and clothing, and waves crashed rhythmically against the pilings, mirroring the confusion within Geri.

"I feel...lost, Andrea," Geri confessed, her voice cracking. "It all seems hopeless. Vance is winning, people are giving up, and I... I don't know if I can do this anymore."

Andrea stopped, turning her brown eyes to Geri's. "Look at you, Geri," she said softly. "You're facing down a powerful man, standing up for what's right, even when it seems hopeless. You are making a difference, even if you can't see it yet."

Geri scoffed, but Andrea continued. "I've lived here all my life, and people here are good, decent folks. Some may be swayed by greed and fear, but down deep, they're good. They value diversity and honor the freedom to be who we are. These are things Vance and people like him cannot destroy."

On their walk back to the coffee shop, Andrea began humming softly. Geri recognized the melody instantly – "Ready to Take a Chance Again" by Barry Manilow.

* * *

Geri was vaguely aware of light seeping in from the window, illuminating her apartment. Elusive sleep was replaced by a searing resolve that chased away exhaustion. She was done with pining for the past, for the life she and Marisol planned for, and then lost. Geri, the unsure college student who'd tiptoed out of the closet, had transformed, and a nascent plan was darting around in her head.

She got out her laptop and sat on the floor near the coffee table. She identified the case's facts, separating them from the guesses and suspicions. If she allowed Vance and Cox to get away with their crimes after putting Armand in the hospital, it would paint a target on everyone in Pride Point. She learned in her job that the insurance business is a people business. She knew she needed to help Armand and the residents of their community.

After a brisk shower and slipping into work attire, Geri paused at her apartment door and reread the quote from the painting. "Okay, Mr. Manilow," she whispered. "My destiny is mine to claim. I won't let anyone else control it. This is my fight, and I won't give up." She took one last glance as she closed and locked the door. "Thank you, Marisol," she thought, her memory now a bittersweet pang mixed with gratitude. "And you, too, Barry."

* * *

Geri flipped on the office lights and, settling into her desk, quickly found an email from Officer Cox with the police report on the bookstore vandalism incident. It was a meager document, lacking details and reeking of disinterest. One terse sentence stated the investigation was closed "due to lack of department resources and low probability of apprehending the perpetrator."

She moved on, discovering that Vance Janitorial Services' insurance policy provided a risk management program that included GPS tracking data on the vans.

Geri accessed the program and pulled up the location history for the van with license plate number VJS 007, revealing exactly what she'd suspected: the van was parked near Armand's bookstore at the time of the vandalism and during the attack on him. She wagered it showed the same pattern for the acts of petty destruction that provoked health and safety code enforcement actions on The Salty Siren and other local businesses, pressuring them to sell. No doubt Cox was the officer writing up those violations.

The evidence was mostly circumstantial, not enough to secure an arrest, especially with potential corruption within the local police department if it went further than Cox. "We need more," Geri thought. A solution occurred to her. She quickly searched for a phone number and called it from her office phone.

"Federal Bureau of Investigation, Special Agent Paula Robinson. How may I help you?"

"Yes, hello," Geri said. "My name is Geri Montesquieu, an insurance claim investigator. I'm calling to report suspected hate crimes and police corruption going on in Marina Vista."

* * *

The tension inside the insurance agency's conference room crackled like electricity as Geri sat across from Special Agent Paula Robinson, a sharp-eyed woman with the confidence and conviction to match her training and years of experience. Geri recounted to Agent Robinson the details of her investigation. She laid out all she had found: the pattern of health and safety code violations against businesses in the Pride Point neighborhood, Vance's pressure campaign to force them to sell to him at rock-bottom prices, the videos and photo of a white van with license plate VJS 007 and a distinctive 'how's my driving' sticker, the insurance file documents linking it to Vance, GPS tracking data showing it at crime scenes, as well as Cox's intimidation tactics, and the suspicious nature of Vance's wealth.

Agent Robinson divulged that Vance had already been on their radar, and she proposed a daring plan – a sting operation.

"We need Vance to incriminate himself," she explained. "Publicly confronting him might force him into a corner, make him lash out or reveal more than he intends." She assured Geri that she would be well protected. The room would have hidden cameras and microphones, with FBI agents stationed discreetly nearby.

Jeri sat stiffly in her chair, aware of her racing pulse. "He's running for city council," she said. "The threat of this story going public might be enough to make him squirm."

Agent Robinson smiled. "Criminals make mistakes, especially when they feel pressured. We need to create the right environment and let him hang himself with his own words. At a minimum, it should get us what we need to open a full-blown investigation."

* * *

The rest of the day was a blur of frenzied activity. Technicians installed hidden cameras and microphones in strategic locations throughout the room, blending seamlessly with the existing decor. Geri rehearsed her role, anticipating Vance's reactions and practicing her questions.

She heard Agent Robinson's voice at the expected time, taut with anticipation. "He's coming."

Geri took a deep breath, forcing herself to remain calm, as the door creaked open, revealing a cocksure Donovan Vance in a slick suit and a trained smile that never quite reached his eyes.

"Ms. Montesquieu," he greeted her with a false cordiality. "What can I do for you?"

Geri gestured towards the seat across the table. Vance took the seat, his eyes fixed on her.

She leaned forward, a file folder clasped in her hands. "Mr. Vance," she began, her voice even, "we've been reviewing your insurance information for Vance Janitorial Services."

Vance scoffed. "Review? Everything's above board, Ms. Montesquieu. My company has an impeccable reputation."

"There are discrepancies, Mr. Vance," she replied. "For instance, the expense of your offices and the revenue figure you've reported… the math doesn't check out."

Vance's smile faltered for a moment, but he recovered quickly.

"What can I say?" he asked rhetorically. "I'm a genius at business."

Geri moved on. "That brings me to another point. The GPS tracking data from your vans paints an interesting picture." She turned the screen on the table round to Vance, displaying a series of maps. "Specifically, the location of your vehicles on the days Mr. Derian's bookstore was vandalized, and when he was assaulted."

Vance's face drained of color. He stared at the screen, his eyes widening in disbelief. The evidence was clear: his vans were near the scene of each crime.

"Perhaps you could explain that, Mr. Vance," Geri queried.

Vance cleared his throat. "It must be a mistake," he stammered. "Maybe a rogue employee or someone using my vans without authorization. It's… a misunderstanding."

Seeing his discomfort, Geri pressed on. "And Officer Russell Cox…" she paused, letting the implication hang in the air before continuing. "We have reason to believe he is involved with extremist hate groups causing violence in our city. The same groups that you are known to associate with."

Vance's face contorted in rage. "Cox? That incompetent buffoon! He messed up the whole thing!" He slammed his fist on the table, the sudden outburst shattering the tense conversation. This outburst was precisely what they'd hoped for – a crack in Vance's facade.

Geri seized the opportunity. "So, you admit what's going on?" She pressed, her voice calm and firm.

"I admit nothing!" Vance glared. "But those so-called extremists, they're just a means to an end. A way to keep these… these freaks in their place!" He spat the word "freaks" with undisguised disgust. "I'm charting a new path for this city."

The air grew thick with hostility when, suddenly, the door swung open with a bang, revealing Officer Cox. He barged in, his face flushed with a mixture of anger and intoxication.

"Vance! What the hell is going on here?" he bellowed, his gaze landing on Geri with undisguised contempt. "You again, troublemaker?"

Vance's face paled. "Cox! I told you… This is a private…."

"Private?" Cox scoffed. "Don't tell me she hasn't squeezed you for hush money yet, huh, Vance? She knows too much about you and your little 'redevelopment project.'"

Geri's expression registered her disbelief. Cox's arrival, an absurd stroke of luck, was turning the tide, his words, a damning confession.

Vance lunged towards Cox in a desperate attempt to silence him. "Shut the fuck up, you idiot!" But the damage was done.

Cox, emboldened by alcohol, shoved back. "Don't touch me! Do you think I will take the fall for you, Vance? For your political ambitions? Those fags and dykes, they're deviants and child molesters that need to be purged from our country, but it's all about the money between you and me!"

Cox's homophobia was sickening. "They're not 'fags' and 'dykes,'" Geri interjected, her voice shaking with anger. "They're citizens of this city."

Cox sneered at her. "Citizens? They're nothing but a bunch of… of…" He trailed off, searching his mind for the most hateful epithet. "They pollute the blood of this city with their filth!"

Vance, now sweating profusely, attempted to regain control of the situation. He reached into his pocket and pulled out a thick wad of cash. "Here, Cox," he hissed. "Take this. Consider it a… bonus."

Cox's eyes lit up with avarice as he snatched the money. He stuffed it into his pocket without bothering to count it. "Alright, alright," he mumbled. "But this isn't over, Mr. Fancy Pants."

The stench of corruption lingered ominously in the room. Cox's actions confirmed their worst suspicions – a twisted alliance between a wannabe politician and a corrupt cop.

Cox's eyes narrowed, turning his attention back to Geri as his hand dropped to the Glock in its holster, resting his palm on the butt. There followed the sound of his thumb unsnapping the strap, a menacing metallic click that sliced through the air, the unleashing of lethal force.

Vance looked over the table, meeting Geri's eyes. "Well," he said in a voice dripping with sarcasm. "I think it's time we acknowledge our business relationship has concluded."

Then, as he stood to leave, he spoke directly to Cox. "Make it look like an accident, a robbery gone bad or something. Use your imagination."

As Cox began to draw his gun, a voice suddenly rang out from behind him.

"Officer Cox, stand down!" Agent Robinson commanded, flanked by three other FBI agents emerging from the hidden doorway. They moved with practiced efficiency, their hands reaching for handcuffs.

Cox froze, his face drained of color. Vance, mouth agape, looked like a fat catfish on a hook.

"You're under arrest, Mr. Vance," Agent Robinson declared. "You are suspected of conspiracy, bribery, vandalism, and assault…and whatever else we find once we delve into your finances."

"And you, Officer Cox," she continued, her eyes fixed on the stunned cop. "You're under arrest for aiding and abetting a crime, accepting bribes, and obstruction of justice."

"And just so you know," she said with a wink, gesturing to the hidden cameras. "This meeting has been recorded and will be used as evidence against both of you,"

The room grew silent after the agents led Vance and Cox away. Geri collapsed back in her chair, tension draining from her body as she let out a long sigh, her shoulders slumping in relief.

She felt the weight of the past few days evaporating, replaced by a cautious optimism. When the news broke about Vance and Cox, it would put the kibosh on his city council election plan and the greedy scheme to destroy the Pride Point neighborhood. A new dawn was breaking for Marina Vista, one free from the shadow of fear and corruption.

* * *

Two weeks later, the sun shone down vibrantly on a late afternoon, having burned away the coastal fog and the remnants of June gloom. Geri strode along the sidewalk, her steps light, her head held high and eyes forward, the handle of her guitar case a reassuring weight in her hand. As she reached the entrance of Surfside Grind, the coffee aroma mingled with the silver tinkle of laughter and spilled onto the street to meet her.

Inside, a diverse crowd buzzed with friendly chatter. Blake and Olivia sat at a table near the front, smiles on their lips, while they and Armand, recovered from the attack and predicted to win election to Marina Vista city council, shared a laugh. Gratitude swept through Geri as she wove through the tables toward the corner stage, her gaze lingering on the faces of the many friends she recognized, every seat occupied, and more people standing against the walls.

With a gentle strum on her strings, Geri stepped onstage with Andrea at her keyboard, who sparkled in a yellow dress, her smile as warm as a summer sunset over the Pacific Ocean. Together, they launched into a jazz rendition of "Ready to Take a Chance Again." Geri's voice, once hesitant, now soared with confidence, harmonizing flawlessly with Andrea's. The cafe fell silent, captivated by the music. As the final notes faded, the crowd erupted in applause. Geri, beaming radiantly, met their cheers with a wave.

Since You've Been Gone

Inspired by *Even Now* from the album
Even Now (1978)

Recita Clemons

I pick up my binoculars in order to track the crowd milling about below my perch on top of Burch Hill. Some peer along the river bank and the rest scope out the edge of the woods.

How dare they come here? This was our place and they have no right to invade it like this. One of the group glances up in my direction and I scoot back into the bushes and out of view. I squeeze my eyes shut and count to thirty. The counting done, I open them again. The people are still there so I place the yellow mums and small, wooden cross on the ground next to me. I shiver under the late morning sun and pull my jacket tight. Even now, I wonder if they'll find you and what they'll do to me when they do.

I lean against an old, dead tree thankful for the cushion my down jacket provides, sip from my thermos of hot coffee and allow the memories to flow.

Our liaison began innocently enough. I, Jill Newell, experienced employee with Ultra-Fast Packing and Delivery, and a close resemblance to the old Oprah rather than the slimmer, newer version was assigned to show the ropes to new hire Raymond Robbins.

In the past, each new employee barely gave me a second glance during my presentation. But not Ray. His deep, soulful brown eyes never left my face.

I invited him to join me for lunch that day, using the excuse to show him the ins and outs of the cafeteria and to warn him to stay away from the salad bar on Fridays and don't even think about trying the lunch meat sandwiches no matter what day of the week.

And so it began.

"So, Jill," Sara had said that first month after Ray's arrival, "we all notice you and the new guy hangin' out a lot. What's happenin' with you two?"

"No idea what you're talking about," I said.

Sara was the number one gossip and I was flattered that after all these years I finally rated a seat at the curiosity table. Ray's attention forced everyone to look at me in a different light and I liked it. A lot.

That first year morphed into the next when each day brought the excitement of seeing him again. To my utter amazement, his attention toward me increased as time passed. I bought new clothes and lost so much weight even my husband Phil ogled me.

Phil and Jill. I cringed every time people made a big deal about how even our names were cute together.

"So, what's going on?" Phil asked one day as I stood in front of our bedroom mirror and tried on a new outfit. "You never wear red. You always said the color made you look fatter than a tick sucking on a pig."

Oh yeah, I thought. But it wasn't me who made the comment. It was mister lite-beer-and-chips-in-front-of-the-TV's favorite line. I tightened the belt around my waist.

I smile at the memory and sip more coffee when a shout rings out and I sit up. The group below grows in size as several people in white rush to join the others. "You're getting warmer," I whisper to myself, "close, but no cigar."

I almost shout "you're not gonna find him" but I keep my mouth shut and remember the brief affair with the man who disrupted my world.

Ray and I played it cool at all the company service anniversaries, office retreats, holiday parties. Nobody suspected a thing, not even our respective spouses.

Last summer Ray and I couldn't stay away from each other. We managed to work side-by-side at every turn. One day, Sara cornered me in the ladies room. "You know your relationship with Ray is getting embarrassing don't you?"

"What on earth are you talking about?" I clamped my lips tight to keep from giggling with glee.

"Don't play coy," she'd said. "Doesn't suit you. This might be hard for you to believe, but that guy's been hitting on every woman not only in our department, but also in shipping. He's playing you, Jill. Open your eyes before you get hurt."

Heat rose up from my neck. "Don't need your advice," I said. "My business is mine alone so I'd appreciate it if you'd keep your comments to yourself." I turned to go, but she grabbed my arm.

I glared at her until she released me.

"I know you and I haven't been the best of friends—"

"Friends? You—and everybody else—rarely acknowledged my existence," I said.

She held her hands up in a stop motion. "True, but I don't want you to get hurt."

"How considerate of you." I washed my hands and let the door slam in her face.

Not long after Sara's warning, my romance with Ray changed forever and came to a head on one hot, July day. Those memories flood back as I squint at the activity below and try to gauge the worker's progress.

Did I hide him behind that large stump? Or several yards in back of that crumbling old stone wall? The precise details grew fuzzier with the passage of time.

My butt aches from sitting on the cold ground, but I need to do one more thing. Inside my backpack I keep a small journal of notes and newspaper clippings from the moment he disappeared.

I remove the flower-covered cloth diary and begin reading the first article. "Raymond Robbins, aged 34, was declared missing by his wife

Alma when he failed to return home two nights ago." The fact that she waited over forty-eight hours to alert the authorities made her their prime suspect which was okay with me.

"Maybe those busy bees down there won't find you and it'll snow early this year and keep your remains out of sight." I cover my mouth, although I know there's no one nearby who can hear me.

"It's all your fault," I said, my breath riding on the cold breeze. "If you hadn't been so awful that last month they wouldn't need to invade our special spot."

I continue to think of this place as "ours". "Even now," I say to the woods and people below, "we know it didn't have to end this way. If only you hadn't been so charming, so special, so...you. If only you hadn't been such a good liar that I believed every word, until the day you made sure I had no doubt of your true intentions."

The alarm on my phone sounds, reminding me I must get home. I head down the hill to my car convinced I'd done a great job hiding you. If I hadn't, some hunter would've found you by now.

Those guys can find anything yet they hadn't stumbled over Ray.

I drive home to the farmhouse I love so much and where I once dreamed of living with Ray. I pull in the drive, glad that Phil's pickup isn't there. I hate to see his face after all the memories that fill my soul about Ray.

The chickens, ducks and mini goats greet my arrival. Phil and I gave up having children years ago, so I settled on providing love to the fur and feathered kind. On my way to the living room the landline phone rings. Instead of letting voicemail take the call I answer. On the other end a woman's voice identifies herself as detective Abigail Meeks of the Burch Police Department. "Miz Newell? I'm calling to see if I can stop by and interview you."

"Interview? About what?" I ask, as if I didn't already know.

"The disappearance of Raymond Robbins," she said. "I need a few minutes of your time to go over some loose ends about his disappearance."

"I've already answered your questions. What do you need now?"

She doesn't answer so I swallow a sigh and agree.

Phil arrives while I'm running the vacuum across the floor. His eyebrows shoot up. "What're you doing? It's not Sunday." He shakes his head and saunters to the living room where the news blares that the police were responding to a tip of where to find the missing remains of Raymond Robbins.

"You hear that, Jill? Somebody knows where your good friend Ray's body might be. What d'you think about that?"

Good friend? I don't bother correcting him. Ray and I were more than friends. For months I thought about packing up and leaving Phil. In fact, I planned on it as soon as I could find someone to take care of the animals. So, until that day arrived, I came home each night and trudged up the steps, heartbroken knowing its Phil I'd see on the other side of the door instead of Ray.

He raises the volume on the set. Ray's not hard of hearing. Oh no. He wants me to hear every word of the news report. Ray's wife, Alma, expresses her doubts that he walked away and instead insists someone murdered him. "Yes, he had a roving eye," she said staring into the camera, "but he always came home to me. Always."

Curious, I tiptoe to the living room.

Ray's wife glares at the reporter and shouts my name. "Jill Newell."

I gasp.

"The cops should look at her again," Alma said. The interviewer plays an earlier recording with a few of my co-workers who hinted that yes, shy, sweet Jill had a crush on Ray. That's followed by the lie that he never cared for me.

The only one who refused to believe I had anything to do with Ray's disappearance was Phil. Good ole dependable, boring Phil. He stood by me no matter what, yet for some reason this year I'd caught him staring at me when he thought I didn't notice. Did he suspect something? If so, why now? Am I acting differently? Were all the questions the cops and the news people asked beginning to take root inside his little brain?

I slide the dust cloth over the side table as the doorbell rings. Deep breaths in...slow breaths out. I knock off any dirt or grass remnants from my jeans, scold myself for not changing clothes, plaster a smile on my face and open the door to a female detective who looks as if she recently graduated from high school. No matter. I've told my story so many times I don't have to think about it anymore.

"Hi," she said, extending a well-manicured hand. "I'm detective Abigail Meeks, Thanks for agreeing to an interview."

I motion her inside and swallow an "as if I had a choice," remark. "We can sit at the dining room table. Ignore my husband. He's watching the game and won't bother us." Last time I talked to the cops, I decided I no longer wanted to offer refreshments to people who seemed hell-bent on making me their prime suspect.

I examine the detective in front of me. This time they send a woman with skin the same deep brown as my own. Maybe they figured this idea would promote some kind of sister-solidarity between us in order to take the sting off trying their best to put me away. I hold her gaze until she looks away first.

"I'll cut to the chase, Jill," she said. "The cold case unit I head up can't resolve some issues with Raymond Robbins' mysterious disappearance."

"What's mysterious about it? One day he's at work and next day he isn't. I'd take another good look at his wife if I were you." How many times, I wonder, are they gonna keep hashing over the same old information while at the same time expecting to get a different result?

"The problem is that we've uncovered a few witnesses—co-workers of yours—who remember how obsessed you were with him and how devastated you were when he insisted you leave him alone."

"Obsessed? Devastated? Me?" Beads of sweat popped onto my forehead. "Who are these so-called witnesses?"

She doesn't answer and the silence stretches on.

"If somebody claims Ray told me to leave him alone, they're wrong."

"According to these employees," Meeks said, "the rumors swirled around you almost from the moment he began work there. These latest witnesses corroborate the others and added that you followed him from work on several occasions and parked outside his house."

"If that were true, where's the proof?"

She gives me a lopsided smile. "The surveillance from the neighbor's house is no longer available."

"And yet, you're accusing me based on rumors?" I want her out of my house so bad my arms itch. Resisting the urge to scratch I steal a sideways glance at Phil. His eyes never leave the screen. Good ole Phil. He never interferes with any of the interrogations, not even to support my version of events.

Meeks waits a few beats before responding. "We found human remains today along Burch Creek. While we don't know for sure who the person is, we have a pretty good idea. We're checking for DNA, so I'd like to give you the chance to tell me what you may have left out of your answers in the past."

I don't speak. Was she bluffing? I didn't see anyone remove anything when I sat on top of that hill.

"I know you've been over this many times," she said, "but I'd like for you to go over when and under what circumstances you last saw Raymond Robbins."

If I ask about the remains would that arouse suspicion?

I let the silence stretch on while I struggle with what to say. My eyes drift toward the ceiling as if that was where the answers lie.

"Tell me about the last time you saw Robbins," she said in a voice barely above a whisper.

Easy girl, don't deviate from what you told the cops in the past.

I clear my throat. "I saw him that day at lunch time. I sat at my usual spot near the microwave, and he and a few friends of his grabbed the largest table near the door." I stop talking. No way was I gonna volunteer information. If detective Meeks wants me to confess to having anything to do with his vanishing, she has another think coming.

"Was lunch the only time you saw him that day?"

I nod and continue. "Didn't see him during work hours. But, that same evening when I walked to my car, he strode over to his convertible. I waved, he didn't wave back and that was that." I shrug.

Her lips curl into a tight smile which doesn't reach her dark eyes. "Let's go back a second. When you saw him in the break room, did you speak to each other?"

"No. I mean, I might've nodded, you know, to acknowledge him. That's the polite thing to do." Based on what he'd done to me that evening I should've received an Oscar for doing that much.

The detective searches through her bag and pulls out a pair of rubber gloves and a tube with what looks like a long Q-tip inside. "Mind if I take a DNA sample from you?"

I expect this. I nod and open my mouth for the swab. DNA away, I think, it won't make any difference.

"Tell me something, Jill," Meeks said. "Why do your co-workers say you might have something to do with why Robbins went missing?"

I lift a shoulder. "Don't know. Guess they never thought a handsome guy like him would pay me any attention."

"How did your relationship end?"

I bristle at the thought. "No relationship, as you put it. We ate lunch sometimes, kidded around—"

"But you admit you liked the attention."

She has me there. "No harm in making friends, detective. And we were only friends."

Meeks hesitates so long I begin to wonder if she has something else up her sleeve. "Do you have any idea who caused his disappearance?"

I glance over at Phil. She follows my gaze. "Do you think—?"

"No. No way." I lower my voice although the volume from the television prevents him from hearing anything. "Leave him out of this. He barely knows what day of the week it is. He goes to work, comes home, helps sometimes with the animals and that's it." I lean in close. "Go back to that wife of his. What woman is truly okay with her husband's flirting?"

"Or with a boyfriend who flirts with others?"

I press my lips tight.

"One of the tips we received but didn't act on at the time, was the sighting of a pickup truck near Burch Lake," detective Meeks said. "No one followed up because it didn't seem relevant. But a tipster said you sometimes drove your husband's pickup. Is that true?"

"This is the country, detective," I said. "I buy feed for the animals and load the food onto the truck bed. Tell me who doesn't drive a pickup in this area?"

I study her face. If she plays poker odds are she won quite a few hands. "Yes, but witnesses said you drove a truck to work that day, not your car."

"They're wrong." I cross my arms.

"Are you sure?"

"Absolutely."

Meeks opens her mouth to say something. Instead, she puts her notepad in her bag. "Thanks for your time Jill. I'll be in touch."

I don't trust my voice so I nod and escort her to the door without another word. I wait until the unmarked sedan pulls off down the drive and onto the road before returning to the kitchen.

"What's that about the pickup?" Phil asks from the couch.

"You heard what she said?"

"My hearings great. You of all people should know that. By the way, in answer to your concern about me not knowing what day it is, today's Saturday. My eyesight's twenty-twenty in case you forgot that, too. And I do recall you takin' the truck out more'n usual. Wondered about that but never mentioned it because you always came right back."

I examine the back of his head and wonder if the answer to how much he knows lay somewhere between the bald spot and the tufts of hair below. He slurps beer and crunches chips and ignores me.

I sit at the table and relive Ray's last day.

He'd started to avoid me a few months before. I thought maybe his wife was getting too suspicious and he wanted to cool things off a bit. But, we were alone in the break room one day when I expressed how much I loved him. Instead of admitting he felt the same, Ray laughed at me.

"Oh, c'mon Jilly. Our fling was all fun and games. More of a friend with benefits kind of thing, so thanks for the memories, babe, but it's time for us to move on."

My hands shook so much I almost dropped my coffee mug. "You said I was special and that you'd never dated anyone like me before."

"I meant I'd never dated anyone your *size* before, though I gotta say you look a lot better now than you did when we first met. But losing all that weight meant now you're like everybody else." He shrugged. "Sorry, but nothing special about you anymore, so chill, Jill. See you around."

I followed him home that evening and several nights after that. I sent texts that he ignored. I even offered to put the weight back on, but all he did was laugh at me.

"Explain somethin' to me, Jill," Phil said, hauling me back from my memories. *Crunch, crunch! Slurp!* "One morning I go out and find my truck cleaner than it was the night before. How'd that happen?"

Nausea takes hold. I close my eyes. The *thump* of tires as it runs over a body once, twice, three times, coupled with the *bump, bump* under the driver's seat each time will never leave me. For the first time I wonder if he suspects what I did.

I didn't plan what happened. Phil saying I could drive his precious truck to work was pure luck. No one was around that quiet, dark night to poke and pry into my business. Nosy Sara called out sick and only Ray and I worked overtime.

We left at the same time.

I wanted to talk to him, explain I understood his desire to end the relationship, and to express my desire to remain friends. He caught me following him and yelled for me to leave him alone and what a loser I was.

Crushed, I climbed into the truck. The engine rumbled to life. Ray swaggered off and I turned the wheel in his direction before I even thought of what I was doing. The shocked look on his face before he fell continues to haunt my dreams.

Lifting his body onto the truck bed wasn't hard. Years of farm work substituted great for workouts at any gym. The drive at night was a piece of cake since I knew these country roads like the back of my hand. I drove to our secret place far away from prying eyes and covered the body with rocks, dirt, branches and leaves.

No matter how hard I tried to forget him, I saw his face everywhere I looked at work; in the microwave glass, across from the assembly line, whenever I passed his locker with his initials still glued to the outside. When I went home and climbed up the stairs to the bedroom I shared with Phil, I imagined I smelled the pine and spice of Ray's cologne.

"So," Phil said, trespassing into my thoughts, "whatcha think about them cops stirrin' up this whole mess again?"

It'll pass the same way it always did, I think. A little noise, stares, pointed fingers, and after a week or two everything will go back the way it was before.

"I'm guessin' this time's different from the others. Seems like findin' them bones will set them in the right direction." He turns around to stare at me. "Does this make you nervous?"

"Why should it? Nothing's changed." I try to swallow, but can't.

"Gotta disagree with you there, sweetie. Everythin's changing this time. This time looks like they got the body." He faces the TV.

I wander to the kitchen and after several gulps of water, find my voice. "If I didn't know better, I'd think you believe I had something to do with this. After fifteen years of marriage, Phil Newell how could you—"

"That new lady detective sounds smarter'n all them others combined."

The lump in my stomach crawls up to my chest. I can barely breathe. I stride over to the couch and stand in front of him. "What're you gonna say when they interview you?"

"Same thing as always, darlin'. That you was here all night long." He motions for me to move out of the way.

I hold my ground. I want to question him about how much he knew about me and Ray. "You believe me, right?"

He pauses so long, I open my mouth to repeat the question, but he answers before I can.

"Nope."

"How...how can you think I could harm him?"

"I thought once you stopped speaking his name all the time like you used to, you'd gotten over him but I was wrong," Phil said, shaking his head over and over.

"I never—"

"I'd hear you cryin' at night."

"That was only because...because the cops believed those stupid rumors. I wasn't obsessed with the man. After all, you're my husband." Even to my ears the words sound hollow. For the first time I suspect he's the tipster.

"When he first...left I wondered what happened. I felt sorry for his wife," I said. "That's the most normal thing in the world."

"Normal. Right." *Slurp, slurp. Crunch.* "Curious about something else, Jilly. How'd you do it?"

My heart sinks. "Do what?"

"You know." He peers at me through heavily lidded eyes.

Tears well up. "I...I've gotta know. Will you be there for me?"

"I'll always support you no matter what. But if you don't confess this accident—or whatever happened between you and him—is gonna eat both of us up."

"You think it...whatever happened was unavoidable?"

"What else could it be darlin'? 'Course that don't explain why you didn't call for help."

"I...panicked. All I could think to do was shove his broken body in the truck bed and hide him until everyone's memory of him faded. I didn't mean to do it." I fall to my knees. "He kept laughing at what a fool I'd been to think we could have a life together. He was right. I was a fool, but I didn't know it then. It was dark. The parking lot was empty. It was almost as if the truck drove itself into him. I...I wasn't thinking of the consequences."

"What did you plan on doin' with me?" For the first time this evening, I hear the pain in Phil's voice and watch the light in his eyes dim.

Tears roll down my face. "I'm so sorry. I wasn't thinking of anything except how numb I'd been because it seemed as if you and I were just going through the motions of a marriage by rote and devoid of feelings."

He shook his head over and over. "We're gonna need to work on some things."

"But what about...what happened?"

"Can't ignore that. You got that lady cop's number?"

I manage a quiet, "yes."

"Give her a call. Tell her you got somethin' important to say. I'll make us a pot of coffee while we wait." Phil strokes my face. "I love you. You know that, right Jilly?"

"Even now? After all that's happened?"

His gap-toothed smile warms my heart.

"Even now," he said.

Bermuda Triangle

Inspired by *Bermuda Triangle* from the album
Barry (1980)

J. M. Taylor

They were halfway through the two hour flight, and Justin felt panic starting to gnaw at his belly. Here he was about to spend a week in the Bermuda sun and surf with this woman—Kaitlin was her name—and he realized that outside of their hefty lust for each other, he didn't know much about her. Sunbaked sex was well and good, but could he keep it up for a solid week? What happened when they they had to emerge from their room and actually face the world?

Small talk didn't come naturally to him. He sipped on his drink, searching for a funny, revealing anecdote. Something sweet, endearing. Innocent.

"When I was in third grade," he told the woman in gazing out the window, "we had this new teacher in the room next door. Looked exactly like Barry Manilow."

"Who?" she said distractedly.

"The new teacher."

"I got that part. Who'd he look like?" When she turned to face him, the light reflecting off the wing lit her eyes just right, but her frown ruined the effect.

"Barry Manilow. And the funny thing is, he had posters of him all over the room. We thought it was his brother or something."

"But who is this Barry person? Should I know him?"

They had never discussed age, and Justin was lucky that he looked younger than his fifty-two years. He'd been carded into his forties. Not that it had helped him much in the romance department. And now that he had a good thing going, he had a glimmer of a suspicion he might be in a cross-generational romance, one that opened up like the Grand Canyon somewhere around the time MTV stopped showing music videos.

"You know, he wrote the songs that make the world sing," he pressed on. "'Copacabana'? 'Mandy'?"

She squinted and tilted her head, and Justin realized that his conversational gambit hadn't panned out, but he was it deep in it now, and had to go forward.

"Anyhow, we were sure it was his brother—same nose, same lips." He sighed, defeated. "Looking back, he probably didn't look at all like Barry Manilow."

"You could've googled him," she suggested.

"Yeah. You're right. Don't know why any of us didn't think of that." He sipped at his drink again and added under his breath, "In 1978."

He settled back in his chair, gave Kaitlin's brain a chance to filter out the awkwardness and remember their plan to make love on the beach under the light of a full moon. Not that he'd checked a lunar calendar, but in his mind there was always a full moon above the crashing surf.

Their romance had been a quick one. They'd met at the gym, maybe a month ago, and Justin was glad he hadn't had to download another app and learn which way to swipe or anything like that. The electricity between them had been sudden and strong, and Justin rose to the occasion. Kaitlin was fun and adventurous, but often busy with her job as a marketer for an online store. It kept her working late, and more than once she'd had to bail on a date, but they always made up for it later.

The plane banked towards the airport, and over Kaitlin's shoulder, Justin watched the brilliant blue sea meet the line of blazing white sand. She turned and smiled at him, and he took her hand. The gentle glide of her fingers on his told him all he needed to know about the relevance of any age gap. Perfect.

The plane touched down and taxied to the gate. The lights flickered on and then the baggage compartments were opening. Justin took down their bags and stepped back to let Kaitlin out. She glanced casually up and down the aisle, then dropped into the seat. Her face was glowing red.

"What is it?" he asked.

Kaitlin laughed. "Nothing, just being stupid. Come on, lover, let's get some fruity umbrella drinks."

They shuffled off the plane and through Customs. All around them, couples that looked a lot like them were huddling together, or quietly fighting, or adjusting themselves. Kaitlin pointed with her chin at one guy who made his way through the line apparently oblivious to all the action. "That's what I was laughing about earlier," she whispered, as if the singleton could hear her. "Forget your Harry Banneville. That guy looks exactly like Mike Evans."

"Really?" Justin craned his neck to see, but the guy had his back to him, and he wasn't about to admit he had no idea who Mike Evans was. "What's he doing here alone?"

"Probably trying to relax after his last shoot." She turned and winked. "Of course it's not really him, right? The real Mike Evans would be mobbed by fans."

Justin wasn't so sure. The crowd around them skewed towards his own age, and if he didn't know the guy, he doubted the others would care, either.

They took a taxi to the resort. Justin was happy they had splurged on the accommodations. Their room opened up onto the beach, and it was steps from a well-stocked bar. They had a stroll on the beach— no full moon tonight—a large fruity drink, and a splendid evening in bed. But he had to admit to himself, a large part of his performance was rooted in desperation. Who the hell was Mike Evans, and why did he make her blush?

On their first full day, they had breakfast on the veranda, mimosas and fruit, and then a dip in the ocean. Kaitlin was resplendent in her bikini, and Justin wasn't too embarrassed by his own shape in his suit. They splashed until the sun grew too hot, and she suggested a drink by the pool.

"Nice idea," he said. "I like the bar *in* the pool."

"Let's do it."

They crossed the sand, and Justin took the opportunity to walk behind her, admiring the swing of her walk. As they entered the pool area, he casually swept his gaze across the faces in and around the pool. Most were paunchy middle-aged couples, but there was a respectable amount of women that would give Kaitlin a run for her money. Not that he was shopping, mind you. She gathered her hair and plunged into the pool, a perfect arrow gliding through the water. He stood on the edge, all set to follow her.

But before he dove in, he noticed that the ersatz Mike Evans lay on a chaise across from them, and he was clearly watching Kaitlin's underwater strokes. When she broke the surface and waved to Justin, Mikey looked up to find his rival. He raised a glass in surrender, and Justin cocked his eyebrow in response.

The swim-up bar was situated so their backs would be to the would-be interloper, and Justin took advantage of that by playing with Kaitlin's hair, caressing her shoulder and back, and once even leaning in to kiss her. Kaitlin was clearly oblivious to the watcher, and in fact when they finished their drink, he was gone.

But now Justin was on the lookout. Over the next couple of days, he caught sight of the stranger at dinner, eating alone, while Kaitlin did a puppet routine with her lobster, and again when they joined in at the midnight dance party. The next day they made an excursion to the sea glass beach, and there he was, dark shades contrasting with the blue and green shards at his feet. Each time Justin clocked him, he was alone, and while he wasn't exactly staring at Kaitlin, or even paying much attention to her, Justin was certain that this character was always aware of where she was.

It wasn't until Kaitlin was in the shower the next morning that Justin had a chance to do any solitary googling—taking a tip from her—to find out about their new shadow.

Turns out Mike Evans, the real Mike Evans, was something of a burgeoning big deal actor. He'd been in a few limited series on streaming platforms, but none that Justin watched. He'd played a hot priest, a police recruit, a crusading lawyer. There was talk he was going to make the leap to the big screen, maybe even in the running to be the next James Bond. But as Justin scrolled through the images, he realized that his guy didn't actually look at all like the rising star. There was a classic chiseled look to the real deal, his hair was lighter, and the lonely guy lurking at the edge of the pool had a definite lack of chiseled abs. What clinched it was that the actor had blue eyes, while the impostor had brown. There was no getting around that.

Not that the doppelgänger lacked vision.

Day three, fake Mike raised the stakes. They were at the pool bar again, and Kaitlin was sipping a massive piña colada. Justin sat to her left, but the married couple on her other side drifted away when they'd finished their daiquiris. You'd think a solo vacationer in need of a drink would skip the stool right next to a clearly un-single woman, but no, he swam right up next to her, ordered his drink from the bartender who looked too young to be slinging shots. At first Kaitlin wasn't aware of him—catching sight of the approaching loner, Justin adjusted his own position so she had to turn more to the left on her stool. But fake Mike was on to him.

"I see one of you is drinking a piña colada, the other a frozen daiquiri," he said, smooth as satin sheets. "I'm not really sure what I want myself. What do you recommend?"

Kaitlin turned her head, and blushed to the edge of the earlobe poking through her damp hair. The guy seemed oblivious, and in fact didn't appear to notice Kaitlin's stuttered response, "Ma-mine's good."

Justin didn't know what was setting her off, since up close this was clearly no Hollywood actor. But the guy had a smile to beat the band anyhow, and when he ordered his own piña colada, he had her attention. So much so, he knew he didn't have to stick around. When he'd been served, telling the bartender his room number for the tab, he swam off with the barest of an acknowledgment that Kaitlin had helped him in his decision. Justin's own drink melted into lumpy syrup, and Kaitlin kept asking, "What? Huh?" as he tried to keep the conversation going.

Finally, Justin kissed her and said, "Let's head back to the room. That suit of yours is driving me to distraction."

It worked, but Justin worried that her mind was very far from him while they made love. When she rolled away from him afterwards, he was sure of it. It was going to be a long week if this kept up.

Then Kaitlin rolled back and gave him a mischievous grin. She draped her leg over his and he realized that he was being ridiculous. She was in love with him, Justin, not some look-alike to an almost famous tv actor.

But the next day, the lonely guy managed to cross their paths at the lunch buffet, and at the line of hotel-owned chairs on the beach. When he showed up five minutes into the salsa class, haplessly partner-less, the instructor told him it was fine, they'd just switch people off. Justin noticed that he wasn't the only one dismayed at his partner's willingness to share. When it was Kaitlin's turn to dance with the loner, Justin was forced, like the other husbands and boyfriends, to grin politely and listen as the instructor pointed out the nuances of the single student's moves.

They were, of course, perfect.

After the class, Justin claimed he was tired. The salsa music banged in his head, and his legs were unsteady as he made his way back to the room. Kaitlin joined him, but when she realized he hadn't been speaking in code, she asked whether he'd mind if she took a taxi and went into town to do some shopping. He told her it was a great idea.

When he woke two hours later, she still hadn't returned. Not that he'd expect anyone to get back so quickly. Maybe she stopped for a bite. He shook the cobwebs from his head, stumbled into the shower. When he was dressed, though, nearly three hours had gone by and he was starved. He checked his phone, but she hadn't left a message.

He went to the beachside bar and ordered a rum. He'd had enough of frozen, fruity drinks. It went down nicely, so he ordered a second one. By his third, the shadows had lengthened across the sand, and the crashing waves echoed dully in his ears. He jumped when Kaitlin embraced him from behind. She smelled of fresh air and island spices and engulfed him like a cloud. "Get me two of those so I can catch up," she said, taking a seat next to him, letting an armful of bags clatter to the sand.

"Where've you been?" he said thickly after she'd knocked back the first rum in a single shot.

"Like I told you, I took a taxi to the market. Look at this bracelet, don't you just love it?" She showed him a string of polished shells tied neatly to her wrist. It jingled like bells when she twisted her wrist.

"Lovely," he slurred.

After the second shot she blurted, "Andy bought it for me."

"Who?" He dropped her hand like it was a poisonous fish.

"You know, the guy from dance class earlier? He happened to be in the market, too." Coincidentally or not, the interloper settled on the other side of the bar and Kaitlin waved to him, jangling the shells. It sounded to Justin like the cowboy cook ringing the triangle and calling out, "Come and get it!"

"I thought you and me were here for a romantic getaway," Justin said, the rum curdling in his belly.

"Of course, cutie," she said, downing another rum that had appeared unordered. The bartenders, Justin thought even in his anger, knew their job. There was a fresh drink at his elbow, too.

"I can't believe you were out with another guy," he said. "What else did he give you?"

"What's your problem," Kaitlin hissed. "You were asleep. What was I supposed to do, sit around waiting? It's not my fault you were pooped after a lousy dance class. And no, he didn't give me anything else. We just had a couple of drinks."

"What?" He gripped her wrist tight enough to scratch it with the shells.

Mike Evans, or Andy, or whoever the hell he was stood up and came around to them.

"Is there an issue here?" he asked. "I can't help but think there was some misunderstanding. My name's Andy Bell." He offered his hand, and Justin forced himself to let Kaitlin go to shake it. He squinted at the man's eyes. Were those contacts he was wearing?

Bell went on, "I didn't mean to cause any trouble. I know Katie's here with you. We just happened to be in the same café and got to talking. You don't think she'd do you dirty, friend. Would she?"

Kaitlin gave him that head tilt again, and Justin was aware that the other patrons were wondering the same thing. He told himself to grin, and shook his head. "No, of course not. My mistake. Thanks for looking after her."

Andy, formerly Mike Evans' evil twin, patted him on the shoulder. "I didn't think so. Take care, buddy." He sailed away like a maitre'd, not that Justin often dined places where he might see one.

"Don't pout," Kaitlin said. "I'd never hurt you. Come on, show me how much you care." She gathered her bags and snatched a bottle from behind the bar, then led Justin back to their room. The three—four?—rums sloshed in his empty stomach and he followed her, not quite sure what had happened, or what his role was in it all. They sat on the balcony and worked through the rum. When Kaitlin suggested they go to bed, he tripped after her, and didn't quite get to show her how much he cared for her.

He woke with a pounding headache, the sun rising across the water. Kaitlin was in the shower. He knocked and let himself into the bathroom. He couldn't wait for her to finish.

"Sorry about last night," he said through the steam. "I feel like an ass."

She poked her head around the curtain, hair hidden beneath a helmet of bubbles. "Don't worry, honey. I get it. You had a couple too many. It happens. Give me a minute, and we'll head out. I have a surprise for you."

"Me?"

"Sure. I just hope you're not prone to seasickness."

Over breakfast she handed him a glossy tri-fold, wrinkled and limp with humidity. The front promised "Glass Bottomed Tours" and depicted a cruiser with two decks, as well as the viewing area inside its hold. The glass was a coffin-sized rectangle between benches in a darkened cabin. Inside, the brochure advertised a cash bar and space for sunbathing during the trip out to see the reefs and wrecks.

"Wouldn't be Bermuda without wrecks," he said aloud.

Kaitlin ignored him and said she'd already reserved places for them that afternoon. "We can look right through the floor to bottom of the ocean. They say we could see all kinds of fish."

"Doesn't sound safe. Can't the glass crack and leak?" He immediately regretted it. Here she was proving to him that not only was he wrong to think she'd done anything with that other guy, but that she was forgiving him for making scene. He couldn't hope for anything more than that.

"What I mean is," he said after a sip of mimosa, "is that it sounds great. Thanks."

"No problem," she said, flipping her freshly-washed hair in the sun.

That's when he saw the red spot on her neck. That wasn't one of his moves, not at all. He chewed his lip and forced himself to smile.

Just like that, he was already formulating a plan.

Kaitlin grinned and planted a kiss on him. He felt nothing but the tingle of champagne lingering on her lips. He stroked her shoulder, but this time it was mechanical, premeditated. If she was going to toy with him like that, well, then, he could play too.

The morning passed in sun and sand and splashing. Justin was every bit as romantic and fun loving as he had been since they arrived, if a bit less drunk. Since breakfast he'd declined his usual day-drinking. "Don't want to fall asleep in the boat." He grinned over their lobster lunch. "But don't let me stop you," he said, ordering her another glass of wine.

As he dismantled his lobster, ripping limb from limb, he studied the image and schedules on the brochure—all in the name of excitement. He timed out the trip, how many drinks he'd buy her, where he'd suggest she catch some rays. As he twisted off the second claw and cracked it open, he settled on a final draft. Just as the tourists would be called in to start their viewing, when all their backs were turned, poor Kaitlin would suffer an intoxicated and tragic fall into the drink. He'd make sure she was incapacitated before she went in. Oh, the horror of it all.

He wrenched the lobster's tail off the body and speared the meat from it in one long piece.

After lunch, they showered and dressed. Justin suggested a drink before they left, so they stopped at the bar. Kaitlin had a shot of rum. Justin had the same, though she didn't notice that he didn't quite get the rum into him. Then they walked to the marina hand in hand. Other couples milled around them, a flurry of color and dark glasses and the scents of half a dozen brands of sunscreen.

The boat was larger than the one on the brochure, but that only improved Justin's plan. There were a number of semi-private spaces along the two decks and in the small bar for people to hide until they all gathered in the dark to watch the fishes.

"Let's find a spot near the back," Justin suggested. He knew there was a proper word for this part of a boat, but he'd never had the occasion to care in the past. If it came to being questioned later, he thought, it might not be a bad thing to come across as clueless.

Kaitlin found them a pair of folding chairs. The sun beat down as the cruiser sped east. The island shrank into the waves behind them, a lush green stripe sinking into the bright turquoise blue. The roar of the two inboard motors made conversation difficult, but Kaitlin nodded when he mimed "Drink?" and he made his way on unsteady land-lubber knees to the bar on the second deck.

When he returned clutching two overpriced beers, Kaitlin was leaning on the rail, letting the wind blow her hair every which way. "You're an angel," she shouted above the roar. She took the beer in one hand, and put her other arm around him. He felt almost loved, and again wondered if he'd misread things. He couldn't even see the mark on her neck, and Justin began to doubt he ever had. Wasn't it on this side of her? He tried to picture what he'd seen at the breakfast table, and now it was lost in the hours and the pounding of the hull against the waves.

"We should do this again in a couple months," Kaitlin said, finishing her beer. "We should do it every year, lover."

"Sounds nice," he answered. "Another drink?"

She giggled, but not quite as drunkenly as he hoped. "Sure, lover. Don't be long."

But the lines for this round stretched to the door. They were closing in on the viewing grounds, and folks wanted to get their last sips in. Standing in line, he watched how one wife was ragging on her husband, who looked for all the world that he wished he'd be abducted by aliens, or mysteriously disappear into thin air. Another couple drank in silence, having run out of things to talk about. On balance, he realized, they'd had a good week together. The "Fake Mike Evans" thing was just a story they could tell later. When he got back to their spot on the rear deck, Justin was certain that he'd been a fool to doubt Kaitlin. They were better off by far than most of the rest of the losers on the boat.

Stepping out into the sun, he blinked and held his balance as the boat veered to the left. At first, he thought Kaitlin had fallen off on her own, since their two chairs were occupied by two entirely different people. Where had she gone?

Then he heard her voice. And saw that Kaitlin was indeed in her chair, along with the absurd actor wannabe. When had he come aboard?

"What the hell is this?" he said, still holding the warming beers. One of them bubbled over with the pressure of his fist.

"Look who signed up for the same trip," she said.

"Didn't mean to horn in on anything," Andy Bell said. "I just happened to be up on the top deck. Imagine my surprise when I looked down and saw Katie here."

"Imagine," Justin said. "Here, take a beer," he said.

"Cheers," Andy said, reaching out.

Without thinking, Justin slammed the other beer-laden fist into his face. Andy stumbled back against the rail, just as the boat banked right—starboard, it vaguely occurred to Justin—and slid unconscious into the water. The motor caught him and there was a brief flash of crimson before the spray gleamed white and blue again.

Kaitlin took a breath to scream, but she never let it out. With another instinctive move, Justin resorted to his original plan, and in one smooth motion tipped her into the water. The surf filled her gaping mouth, and she went under in a flash.

It was another five minutes, when the captain was announcing it was time to go below, that Justin raised the alarm that Kaitlin had gone overboard. By that time, they were far from where the bodies had gone in, and he never said a word about Andy Bell.

The search turned up nothing. Justin cried through the police interviews, but they could find nothing to charge him with. It was all so sudden and sad. He went home when they let him, a day earlier than planned. No more sun for him.

When the news broke, Justin said to himself, "Imagine that? Then maybe that teacher really was…nah, couldn't be."

He'd been back home long enough for his tan to fade when TMZ announced that actor Mike Evans, rumored to be in the running to be the next James Bond, had not been seen in over a week. His partner, Val Peterson, told reporters he was researching a role in Bermuda when he disappeared.

Justin scrolled through his phone as he sauntered past the gym to enjoy a fruity drink instead. "Evans was another victim," the outlet added, "of the mysterious Bermuda Triangle."

Lonely Together

Inspired by *Lonely Together* from the album
Barry (1980)

John M. Floyd

A tall man in a business suit and an attractive woman in a long black dress, both holding drinks, stopped drifting and faced each other beside the crowded bar of one of the city's most elegant nightclubs. After a few words and several long gazes they left the bar and took seats together at a small table in a corner. On the dance floor, two dozen people swayed to the music of a five-piece band.

"I assume, from your accent, that you are American," the woman said.

The man smiled. "And you're Russian."

"Yes, I am. Allow me to welcome you to our country."

He nodded his thanks and studied her a moment. "How do you know I haven't already been here a while?"

"I am making another assumption," she said, returning his smile. "Tell me, are you here for business or pleasure?"

"Business. Forgive me, but I've found very few things pleasant in Moscow."

"I am sorry to hear that."

"Between you and me," he said, leaning forward across the table, "compared to Russia, America is a paradise. No offense intended."

"No offense is taken. But I assure you, there are pleasurable things here. For example,"—she focused on his glass—"what are you drinking?"

"Vodka. How about you?"

"Medovukha. Would you like a taste?" The woman handed him her glass, and he handed her his. He took a healthy swallow, then turned to look at the band as they started up a new song. She sipped from his glass and watched also. For several moments neither of them spoke. It was cozily dark in their corner.

"Not bad," he said, giving her drink back. "Meedabooka?"

She handed him his. "Medovukha. I would rather have tea, actually."

They stayed silent for a while, listening to the music. Outside a window near their table, snow was falling.

Finally she said, "It occurs to me that you have not told me your name."

"Jones," he said.

"Jones?"

"Lonely Jones."

She nodded and smiled. "I see. You do not want to tell me."

He shrugged. "You haven't told me yours."

"I am Lonely Joan," she said.

"Nice to meet you, Joan."

Several seconds passed. Finally she said, "Let us try this, then: If I might ask, what is it that you do?"

"For a living?" He hesitated for only a second. "I'm an intelligence agent."

"Really." She smiled again. "You mean, like how do you say, a spy?"

"One might put it that way, yes. For my government."

"That does sound lonely."

"It is." He sighed and shook his head. "The things we do for our countries, right?"

"I suppose," she said. "So, Mr. Jones—do you have a gun?"

"What do *you* think?"

She tilted her head. Her earrings caught the light, gleaming magically. "Show me."

Watching her face, the tall man opened his suit jacket just enough to reveal the grip of a small pistol in a shoulder holster.

"Ah," she said, eyes mischievous. "Do you think you will need to use that, tonight?"

"I hadn't planned to."

"What a relief." She set her drink glass down and carefully smoothed the tablecloth in front of her. After a pause she looked at him and said, "Gun laws are strict, here—I assume you have a permit to carry that."

"I do."

"I thought permits were issued only to hunters," she said, "for the purpose of hunting."

"The rules were relaxed a bit, two years ago. Since Twenty-Fourteen, foreigners can carry handguns if it's for self-defense."

Another smile. "Am I also to assume, then, that your self is in need of defense?"

"One never knows," he said.

The woman didn't reply to that. Thirty feet away, dancers glided and swiveled and dipped to the music.

"How is it," she asked him, with a raised eyebrow, "that you know so much about our laws?"

"I don't," he said. "My agent does. He acquired the permit, before I arrived."

"Your agent? I thought you were an agent."

"We both are. He's what we call my controller. I'm an operative."

She leaned back in her chair, pursed her lips, studied him carefully. "So what else does this 'controller' do for you?"

"He gives me what I need, to perform my job."

"Instructions, you mean?"

"Among other things." He took a small paperback book from an inside pocket and held it up for her to see. On the cover were the words *Moscow Travel Guide 2016.*

"Ah. Sensitive material, that." She smiled, looked down, seemed to examine the backs of her hands a moment—she wore no jewelry—and said, "And what, exactly, does an operative...operate?"

The man replaced his guidebook and shrugged. "Not much. The remote for my hotel TV, mostly. As you know, the Cold War is less chilly now."

"The Cold War is over. And I agree, things are better now than they were fifty years ago. But the unease is still there."

"Yes," he agreed also. "Still there."

The two regarded each other for a minute in the pleasant dimness. Outside, headlights and taillights drifted silently past. The band started in on "Maria."

"Why do I get the feeling," the man asked her, "that you already knew who I was?"

She looked puzzled. "A feeling?"

"Yes. A strange feeling. Sort of a tingle, in my stomach."

She seemed to give that serious thought. "Perhaps it is the vodka. Or travel sleep disorder."

"Excuse me?"

"Jet lag," she said.

"Perhaps. Or maybe just loneliness."

"Then that makes two of us," she said.

Both of them smiled.

After another silence he looked at the band and said, "Do you know the six elements of drama?"

She frowned. "What?"

He turned to face her. "Aristotle's elements of drama. He wasn't just a scientist, you know. He also studied history, economics, the human mind—especially the arts."

The woman propped an elbow on the table and rested her chin in her palm. In some way she made it look elegant. "Is that so."

"It is. And he decided that every drama has six elements: plot, character, diction, melody, spectacle, and thought."

"Melody?" she said. "Spectacle?"

"Yes—melody as in music, rhythm, something to keep things moving. And by spectacle he meant place, or setting. We have both of those here tonight, you see, for our little drama."

"How interesting. Go on."

"Well, we also have three more elements. The characters—you and I. The plot—we've met, we're sharing a table and drinks, and we're enjoying ourselves. As for diction, or dialogue—we're conversing. Talking. Sharing information. That's five, in all."

"And number six is…"

"Thought," he said. "That's the one we're missing. We don't know for sure what each other is thinking." He grinned at her again, an open, confident, amused smile.

She said nothing. On the other side of the room, the band was taking a break. So much for the music element. The man didn't seem to notice.

Then, slowly, his face changed. "Tell me, Joan," he said to her. "What is it that *you* do?"

"For a living?" Her smile returned. "I am an assassin."

"Really. You mean, like, a hired killer?"

"One might put it that way, yes. For my government."

"That does sound lonely."

"It is," she said.

He glanced at her tight dress and tiny handbag. "I can't help wondering," he said, "where you keep *your* gun."

"I am not carrying one, tonight."

"What a relief."

Another tilt of her head. "But there are other kinds of weapons."

Their eyes held for several long seconds.

"Show me," he said.

She sat perfectly still, her smile intact, her small hands clasped now on the table in front of her. He was motionless also, and seemed in no way disturbed by what she'd said.

Slowly, carefully, she looked at her glass, then at his, then at him.

He followed her gaze: her glass, his glass. Then he looked at her.

And fell forward onto the table.

A nearby waiter, apparently unsurprised by the sight of a customer lying facedown on a tabletop, gave the woman a questioning look. She stood, picked up her coat and purse, returned his stare, and shrugged.

"Medovukha," she said.

* * *

She strolled casually away from the table and through the crowd, her half-full drink glass hidden beneath the coat draped over one arm, and paused only to set the glass down beside several others on one of the empty tables. No one was watching her and no one seemed to have paid her any attention at all. She was almost to the door when she saw her supervisor, Colonel Baranov, emerge from the men's room. He stood there a moment, adjusting his cuffs, studying his surroundings with a practiced gaze. Somehow his bearing and posture made his tailored business suit look like a uniform. Their eyes met, and he beckoned to her.

"My dear Irina," he said, in a low voice. "I saw you, a short while ago. What brings you here?"

"I had heard earlier that the spy Daniel Ross might be present tonight, Colonel," she said, with a glance at the far corner of the room. All still seemed normal, there. People chatted, dancers danced, drinkers drank.

The colonel frowned. "I do not think so. If Ross *was* here, would you recognize him?"

She smiled and raised her chin. "Of course I would. As a matter of fact—"

"If it helps," he said, "Ross looks a bit like that fool you were sitting with, earlier."

Irina blinked. "What?"

"The American film star. Michael something. I understand he is here in the city to shoot a movie."

She stared at him blankly.

"A competent actor," he continued, "but by all accounts, rather strange. My daughter is an avid fan."

Dazed, Irina swallowed and took a long breath. *An actor?* Her mind was spinning.

The colonel seemed to see, for the first time, the handbag and coat she was carrying. He looked at them, then at the front door, then at her face. "Were you about to leave?"

Things *were* changing now, she noticed, in the back corner. A waiter was leaning over her table and motioning urgently to someone. Puzzled customers' heads were turning. Watching all this, three things occurred to her: one of them was that she should've paid a bit more attention to that last element of drama. And the earlier mention of an agent. An *agent*? The third thing, however, was an idea—and right now she badly needed an idea.

She straightened her back and said, "Colonel, I was about to phone you. I am indeed leaving. I have just learned, moments ago, that Daniel Ross is in Washington, D.C."

He stared at her. "What?"

"I have received word that Ross has targeted our ambassador there. At our embassy."

"You mean Nikolai? My cousin?"

"I am afraid so." Holding her breath, she said, "I request permission to depart tomorrow."

* * *

Outside in the snow, Irina couldn't stop trembling—and it had little to do with the weather. She knew the mistake she'd just made and the lie she'd just told were unforgivable, as were the political and media firestorms ahead. But she also knew Colonel Baranov was fiercely protective of his family, including cousins, and that it would be half a day or more—time she desperately needed, in order to close accounts and withdraw savings—before the authorities found out it was poison that had killed the unfortunate movie star and were able to piece it all together. By then she'd be packed up and long gone, never to return. She kept remembering the tall actor's words: *America is a paradise.*

She hoped that was true.

When the Sun Rises

Inspired by *Let's Take All Night (to Say Goodbye)* from the album
If I Should Love Again (1981)

T. Fox Dunham

Just take it out. Don't point it at anyone. Let their imagination do the rest.

Oliver adjusted the lampshade covering his face like he was off to a party then joined the queue along the rope guides behind a customer asking a pharmacy tech why her prescription cost so much when she had insurance.

"Your insurance will only cover the generic," said Maria-the-tech then shut her down with the ubiquitous phrase. "Call your doctor's office." Oliver growled beneath the ridiculous yet easily accessible disguise while the system robbed another of dignity, of basic humanity, assuaging any doubt and anxiety about what came next. Finally, the customer surrendered, stepped out of line then wandered in a daze out of the Pharm Mart. Oliver slowly walked to her place; however, unable to employ his black aluminum cane since it would give him away in a lineup, he stumbled over his numb left foot, and neuropathy nearly ended his career as a cancer outlaw before it began. No one noticed— lampshade and all—and he recovered then faced Maria-the-pharmacy-tech who never really looked up from behind the aegis of her monitor.

"This isn't like declining a credit card," he said, his voice muffled through the thick fabric shade. "The woman just learned that society doesn't value her life.

"Name and date of birth?" Maria said, deflecting his admonition. A lone security camera hung limp from its perch, nor did its little light flare red. Cobwebs covered the corners; water stained through the left wall of this shithole; and a lone, overworked pharmacist rushed to collect bottles from the shelves and funnel pills into orange bottles. Tick, tick, tick the tablets plucked the plastic, and Oliver overheated, diminishing his concentration. He nearly retreated, just like he had with everything in his life, but he was out of time in an existential way and realized this was his last chance.

They couldn't do anything to him anyway, not anymore.

Oliver took out the quaint pistol but only showed it to Maria-the-tech. "I ain't got nothing to lose," he said. "And only the night to gain." The moment washed over him, making him dizzy, but Oliver still couldn't believe it. He'd pulled the trigger—well, without actually pulling the trigger—and he couldn't help thinking that the whole ordeal—getting sick, meeting Jackie, planning a robbery—would have made a best seller, a book he felt finally ready to write; however, as with most good things in life, the conviction, the self-confidence arrived late—as with love.

* * *

A week ago, they took their usual diner booth—a ritual to survive the night through each other's company—and Oliver reverted to his fundamental proclivities, nearly wrecking their coping mechanism when he declared his 'undying' love for Jackie. "You've got the prednisone wack-e-roonies," she scoffed.

"Cancer patients can fall in love," Oliver said then propped his black aluminum cane up against the diner booth wall and took off his ostentatious tan Fedora—bought from a New Hope store called Love Wins the Day—revealing a shadow of bristles growing on his scalp. The store sold mostly nostalgic garb, and he'd also picked up an authentic brown British Burberry, which he wore to cover up his emaciated frame.

"It's the waste of our energy," she said then rubbed lotion into her left stump where surgeons had amputated her tibia.

"It's the only smart thing to do with the time we have left."

"It's too hard to say," she said. "Like goodbye." Shannon-the-waitress bumped into Jackie's wheelchair then plopped down two porcelain mugs of burned coffee at the table. "We don't have a future where it can thrive," she said.

Oliver stirred with a spoon—and stirred and stirred, anything to keep his fingers occupied so they didn't keep groping his neck, feeling the marble poking through his chin. "We have the desperate night," he said. "It's such a great story. Living with death makes love real. We have to. Who we were before. How cancer changed us. How we met." Conversation distracted in the chemo circle at the clinic while pumps infused toxic chemicals. In the denial-world, the two lonely divorcees would have never have bonded; however, proximity and desperation compelled them to forge connection, and they'd always share a struggle that had consumed them mind, body and soul—not that *always* was going to be very long. "I should write it all down," he said and took out his little notebook full of the story ideas he'd gathered over the last two decades since he decided he wanted to be the next Salinger at age ten, though not one story seed had ever gotten beyond the idea stage. He'd been waiting for the right moment, waiting for the right words to come.

"You're a fucking child," she said but looked wistfully out at the parking lot through a pair of oversized tortoiseshell sunglasses, and Oliver tried to see what she was looking at. The last of the residual snow, the gathered gritty and greasy mountains deposited in parking lot corners of the Waiting Diner, corner of Purgatory Street, melted by daylight but sheltered in nocturnal stasis. The actual name of the diner read Waiting to See You Diner, but sections of the illuminated sign on the brick building had long since failed. "Put away the pen," she said then bushed away the chestnut locks from her ratty wig. "Love. Need. Vanity. Be here. Just be with me tonight. This night. It's pointless to count the days."

He finished writing down the idea, put away the book then mourned the death of history. Cancer assaulted from all flanks, consuming their days with doctors, tests, treatment, symptoms, suffering, forcing them to cling to a tiny island of night where in the dark they held back the dark—at least for a time. Most at thirty surrendered youth, started families and built careers; however, Oliver's relapsing lymphoma pushed the needle across the record, so now he prepared to surrender life, bid farewell to his estranged family and lamented a career. "I wasted so much time when I should have been writing."

"I'm not saying those words to you," Jackie said. "I shouldn't have to."

"*Quel dommage*," he lamented. Her phone chimed again, and she grumbled when she read her daughter's fifth text of the night. Her ex-husband served another seven years in prison, and she lived with her daughter while Oliver rented a house with two other divorcees, taking turns sleeping on a futon. "You are getting the biopsy done Friday?" she asked, always bringing it back up.

"I postponed," he lied.

"Father, Son...and holy shit," she said, poking at her flaccid french toast. He'd noticed she'd stopped eating a week ago but probably kept ordering out of habit, just going through the motions. "Don't you want to know how much time we have left?"

"It's liberating not knowing," he said. "All we need is the night. This time. This time now. Tell me one good reason why we shouldn't just let ourselves fall?"

She sighed then dug through the tatters of her designer Moldeo bag for ChapStick. "The Lord gives me just enough strength to endure but not enough to be missing you too." Oliver sensed her pulling away, and he squeezed the foam handle on his cane. He always pushed when he should have waited according to his ex-wife. "My daughter needs me to watch my grandbabies. Physical therapy twice a week. Hours on the phone with Medicare. And always another pointless appointment."

He couldn't blame her. You didn't fight cancer. You endured treatment, and minimizing suffering became your raison d'être.

"If we weren't living in this world of sickness. Could you?"

"My answer will only make it worse."

"Please," he pleaded, but she just sighed.

"Not in this world."

"We'll runaway together," he said, squeezing his cane, desperate for some way to align the great cosmos to his needs. She tilted her head and gazed at him over the tortoiseshell frames.

"Wait?" Jacks asked. "You're serious? Just drop everything for some adolescent romantic bullshit? What about our doctors?"

"The biopsy's a fait accompli—if not now, then soon. Chemo might win me a couple of months of puking, pain, doctors, tests, insurance companies and my children's eternal resentment."

"It's what's expected of us," she said.

"Then let's fuck with this faceless collective."

"You need to remember the rules," she said and started to shuffle the deck of cards. "We have each other only in the night. When dawn comes, cancer owns us again."

"Alaska. The cold dark jewel of the north. Six-week nights lounging on a chilly beach. *Adieu soleil!* We'll take all night to say goodbye."

She shook her head, dislodging the bulbous sunglasses. "My insurance is fighting me on hospice care. I owe over ten thousand in hospital bills. The feds always said my rat shit ex-husband had a secret vault full of money somewhere, but I wouldn't be living like this."

"*Quel dommage,*" Oliver said. "I thought they paid for hospice."

"They want me to do it at home, but I am not putting my daughter through that."

"*Connards!*"

"Save your French. You're so damn pretentious. I've got a family lawyer dealing with it, though I'll be dead by the time they straighten it out. Probably intentional."

"How do you have money for a lawyer?"

"A family lawyer," she said then sighed again.

"Lucky to have a lawyer in the fam'."

"No," she said "He's a *family* lawyer. Friend of my ex-husband's—

may he rot in prison."

She'd only ever hinted at her life before, but from what he could glean on the web, Jacks' ex-husband had been connected to the Philly crime family—an association that had landed him in prison for two decades. He'd gotten pinched while hijacking a truck with flatscreen TVs, and his associates ratted on him for also dealing narcotics. At the time, Oliver had wondered how anyone could risk long swathes of their liberty for quick cash; however, both desperation and mortality had adjusted his perspective, and street legends of her husband inspired.

"I can get to the bus stop on my own," she said, putting down several dollar bills, quarters and dimes then assembled her ragdoll purse and started wheeling herself away from the booth.

He panicked, would have said anything to keep her there. "We could rob this diner."

* * *

They huddled in the bus shelter discussing the inevitability of Oliver's desperate impulse, and even though the clock struck two a.m., his mind raced, awake, alive and desperate to hold onto her. "Father, Son and holy shit," she said, parked next to the tiny bench inside the menu-papered hovel on Duke Street at the edge of Ewell Square. She cradled the purse, making sure it's thousand rips weren't finally going to give, and he squeezed his cane, feeling the dull ache expand in his chest. Junkies slept in the alleys, and bums snored in the tent city they'd erected around city hall.

"I don't want to die in this shit city," he said. "I know it sounds crazy, but things feel different now. It's like us. The way I feel about you." Before the tumor, he patrolled his emotions like a litigious traffic cop, but living with cancer had ripped apart his meticulously crafted walls and avenues. Now emotions flooded, and he felt both grateful and resented being freed of his restraint.

She sighed, opened a pill bottle and swallowed a tiny white mote. "My happiest times were when my grandparents took me crabbing near Ocean City. It's what I hope is waiting. My daughter promises she'll take me one day."

"Every dime I make doing web design goes to my medical bills or child support. I don't even have life insurance. Why would I? I'm thirty."

"SSI pays shit," she said. "I have to sell my meds sometimes."

"*Mon Dieu,*" Oliver said, clutching the foam handle. "That's a thing? How?"

She leaned in and whispered: "One of my ex-husband's 'associates' buys them, sells them to Cuba or something. I take the bare minimum dosage and fence the rest. It's the only way I can pay for the meds at all. Never pain meds. I need extra MSIR for my po' hospice plan."

"Makes...sense." Before all this, he would have been horrified at her confession, but surviving in the world of the dying, struggling just to stay for another day, he'd come to realize you couldn't judge a cancer patient by the same standards for trying to survive. "I could start selling mine too. We could use the money to get out, find something divine and be with each other free."

"We'd never sell enough before our...deadline."

"Then what about my idea?" he asked. At first, it had been an impulsive joke, but this late in their night, desperation normalized the extreme. Sans consequences, they only had to worry for their eternal souls since temporal matters no longer felt relevant.

"No one pays with cash anymore," she said, shooting down his logic.

"Rob a bank?"

She blew raspberries, and her sunglasses nearly flipped right off. "We can barely get to our appointments. Or do you think Medicare will pay for a getaway taxi?"

"It could work."

"What's the point? There's no way we don't get caught."

Oliver sighed and clutched his cane just knowing he was going to fail her like he'd failed his ex-wife, his kids...himself, and Jackie studied her pill bottle in the sallow light. "Could you take me over to Pharm-Mart when they open at five? I need a refill. Got to pay my deductible."

"Fucking deductible."

* * *

"There's no dignity waiting in line," Jacks said then refined the dark chestnut curls of her wig in a makeup display mirror. In front of them, a threadbare mother argued with Maria-the-tech over the shocking price of her prescription—a scene Oliver had often seen play out and always end the same way. Eventually, the line moved up.

There is a call for the pharmacy on line three. There is a call for the pharmacy on line three.

"We have one prescription waiting for you," Maria said after getting Jackie's information.

"Should be two."

"Let me see," Maria said, drumming keys carefully with her pink-painted talons. "We had to order the Duragesic 100s."

"I'm on my last one."

"We get our next shipment on Thursday," the tech said, hiding behind her monitor. Boxes and boxes of craved pharmaceuticals always arrived on Thursdays—one pill to make you think fast, another to keep you tumescent while another melted the weight.

Jackie had no choice but to acquiesce. She knew the game. If she fought the tech, they might thing she was a junkie and find reasons to never fill the prescription; thus, she was a good little cancer patient and accepted waiting for the prescription then fed credit card after credit card into the reader trying to pay. Finally, Oliver made up the difference with his last few dollars.

"I didn't ask you to do that," Jackie said.

"Can you at least call—" Oliver started asking, but one of his meds sometimes dried out the membranes on his tongue. "Call around to other pharmacies and see if they have it?" he asked trying to talk through a mouthful of peanut butter.

"Take a seat," the tech said.

"They hate when you ask them to call around," Oliver said, slurring against his sandpaper tongue. Store policy forbade pharmacists giving out information about narcotic supplies, so patients couldn't call themselves.

"Are you having a stroke?" Jacks asked.

"Side effect," he said.

"Let's get you a soda," she said.

"I'm broke. Child support."

"Push me to aisle three," she said, and he did, stopping in front of an embedded refrigerator.

"Ginger ale? Lemon lime? Orange?"

"I don't have two dollars and fifty cents," he said, and she sighed, adjusted her wig, pushed back her tortoiseshell glasses then casually slipped two cans into her Moldeo purse.

"Floor it."

"We...we can't," he said.

"No one's looking at us. No one wants to look at us."

"You're more beautiful than I can endure."

"Do you need anything else?"

He rattled off a wish list—everything from ibuprofen to fungus cream—and aisle by aisle, they fed her bag. With each item purloined, his heart fluttered. Then, the bag teeming with their stolen goods—everything he needed to be comfortable, to assuage all the little symptoms and twitches and itches—they faced their escape through the automatic doors. Signs warned shoplifters with handcuff icons, threatening their fate.

"Just push me through," she said.

"The sensors will scream."

"It's probably older than I am. Come on, wuss."

"What if we get caught?"

"What's the worst that can happen? They put our asses in jail for the rest of our lives?" She laughed then grabbed his fingers that grabbed her handles, and he braced himself, made sure his black aluminum cane fit snuggly into the holder at the back of the chair then leaned on the chair to support his damaged leg, pushing her to the gate. He tried not to look suspicious, speeding up, slowing down, acting casual. He even thought about waving as he left. A guilty guy shoplifting wouldn't wave, would they?

"Be cool." He pushed her to the threshold. Nothing buzzed, and the door opened. Not one clerk looked in their direction. He kept pushing, maneuvering through the parking lot, waiting for the police, but she was right. They'd been enchanted invisible to the rest of the death-denying world. Finally, they emerged in the early morning light, and he nearly yawped in victory. "We were so obvious!"

"They put their cancer-blinders on," she said.

"This would make a great story," he said. "And it's a proof of concept."

"They can't touch us anyway," she said, handing him a cold soda. "Thursday?"

"Thursday," he said, and the chilly carbonation melted the dried sand burning his throat.

* * *

"You didn't bring a stickup mask?"

"There's no tutorial for armed robbery," Oliver said.

"We'll do this in another week."

"We can't assume we have another week," Oliver said then dug through boxes and furniture deposited by a dumpster. He couldn't screw this up, not this one last thing. He kept digging, going through the boxes of old books, stuffed animals, children's clothes until he found a lampshade. It just fit over his gourd. "It's hard to see through, but it'll work."

"We're so fucked," Jackie said, and Oliver strolled into the Pharm-Mart while she waited in the alley.

"I'm not going to screw this up. I'm not going to—"

"We're very busy today," Maria-the-tech said to him as she studied a break in her obnoxious nails.

"I'm just here to pick up some meds," Oliver said. Sweat soaked through his black sweatshirt, and his heart galloped from his terror, leaped at his exhilaration. He wanted to both run and cheer at the same time.

"Mood stabilizer?" Maria asked, glancing at his clever but improvised disguise.

"I didn't plan this well." He attempted to growl as he spoke, disguise his voice.

"Name and date of birth?" Nothing disturbed Maria, though it disturbed him she wasn't disturbed; so, he showed her the pistol while making sure he didn't aim it at anyone.

"Mother Mary," Maria said.

"*Pleine de grâce,*" he prayed.

"They're going to put you away for a long time—years just gone from your life."

"*Quel dommage,*" he said, laughing then slipped her a typed notecard.

The tech read the list then delivered her perfunctory dialogue like it was a mundane transaction: "I'll have this ready for you in a few minutes." She and the pharmacist filled the sack full of non-life-saving goodies while the people in line behind him gleefully filmed the scene.

"Do you have your insurance card?"

"Nice one. Can I assume you hit a hidden alarm?"

"Try not to damage the boxes," she said, probably assuming the police would soon return the meds, and Oliver grabbed the sack then stumbled for the exit, nearly tripping over his numb foot. The automatic doors opened. Crisp primaveral air cooled his hot skin, and he was about to stumble to freedom when a bull of a bald customer unholstered a big-ass honking handgun and fired thrice from the pantry aisle. The recoil must have surprised him, throwing off his aim because one bullet shot straight through a register, setting off an explosion of sparks.

"Fucking watch it!" Maria-the-tech said. Two more hit the back wall behind the front counter, taking out a row of vaping products and nicotine gum.

Oliver stopped, aimed the pistol at John Wayne and growled through the lampshade. "What the fuck do you think you're doing? You're just making things worse!"

The cowboy dropped his gun then vomited into the Cup-O-Soup shelf, and Oliver hauled ass just in time to hear sirens. He ran back around the back of the store into the surveillance blind spot—they hoped—and tossed the lampshade over the fence. Then, he walked calmly to the other side but neuropathy wrecked his balance, throwing him into a brick wall. Then, as the adrenalin ran out, pain, fatigue flooded his body, but he got back on his feet, reached Jackie and dumped the goods into her torn designer purse. He'd just put on his normal '40's dashing attire, which she'd kept, when cops wearing grey shirts and black vests swarmed the store. The static and squawk of their radios scattered the birds.

The LPD fanned out while cruisers cruised the alleys, and Oliver and Jackie just gawked—a couple of wretches counting their social security payments while eating cat food casserole. Then, his big scene arrived.

"Can I see some ID," asked a uniform—couldn't have been more than twenty, full head of curly dark hair, perfect skin. Oliver nearly reached out and touched him, so free of blemish or disease, so vulnerable. *Don't look at the bag. Don't look at the bag.* He knew she kept her wallet in there, but she couldn't open it in front of the cop without exposing their loot. "I need yours too, ma'am."

"Well, let me see," she said then held the bag up to her face and plumbed its depths. "I don't think I grabbed it this morning. You're welcome to come back with me, cutey. I could really use someone with strong hands to rub castor oil on my back."

"That won't be—"

"Shouldn't you be catching this diabolical *enfoiré* instead of wasting your time among the lepers?" Oliver asked, taking back his wallet. As he hoped, the cop had given up on looking at Jackie's ID, and she lowered the bag; however, he noticed that one of the larger rips spread its legs and exposed a box of Ubik tablets.

"Did you see the perp come out of the store?"

"Sure did," Oliver said, and Jackie kneecapped him with a crowbar-glance. "I mean...what's a perp?"

"The guy who robbed the store."

"Came running straight by us. I thought about tripping him but I can't feel much below my shins. Last time I fell, snapped my wrist."

"Did he look...weird to you?"

"That's a subjective question," Oliver said. Sweat soaked through his shirt. "Looked normal to me."

"He wore a lampshade on his head," the cop added, and both of them shrugged. "Well, if you need a witness for court, I've got two, three months tops. Cancer." Oliver invoked the devil, and the cop handed him his contact card then started back to the store. Oliver nearly collapsed.

"Castor oil?" Oliver whispered, and Jackie shrugged again.

"Oh ma'am," the cop said. "Is that an Orlandi original, made in Milan?"

"A Moldeo original."

"Gorgeous seams," the grunt said, and Oliver rolled his eyes. Of course, the one cop who paid any attention to them was a designer purse enthusiast. "My grandmother had three."

"I've had it for years," she said.

"It's seen better days."

"Haven't we all?" she said, trying to tilt the purse to the side, hiding the exposed box. "Email us if you remember anything." He turned to leave down the alley, and Oliver fell against the brick wall, deflating, then pushed his fists against the tears. Victory! By this time next week, they'd be sitting on some beach and toasting the moon with rum. He knew the night wouldn't last forever, but they'd make the most of their time alone, just the two of them. Life hadn't been perfect, but you had to make the best of it.

"Oh, just one more thing," the cop said, turning around and pointing at the purse "Do you have a prescription for Ubik?"

* * *

"So, the DA felt sorry for us?" Oliver asked. "No trial date?" He shut the patio door behind him, flopped into the beach chair and picked up his drink. He loved rubbing his finger tips on the chilly condensation that pooled on the glass, and he savored the taste of the rum, the aroma of pineapple and coconut. The sound of the ocean waves calmed his turbulent spirit, filled his heart, flooded his vacant depths. One day soon when the tide went out, his soul would release its hold on his broken and spent body and flow back out with it to sea. Then, he'd merge with forever.

"Prednisone made you crazy," Mr. Marino said then adjusted his suit jacket. "They're going to let you run out the clock on bail. I mean, you know."

"It's fine," Oliver said. "I know I'm dying. I think of little else."

"Bad luck—but not all bad. The security system didn't work, and the abused staff enjoyed seeing Pharm-Mart embarrassed."

"I wrote Maria a letter and thanked her," Oliver said, regretting the danger he put her in.

"Social media thinks you're Jesse James with cancer, and your Gofundme will take care of the fines for the lesser offenses plus your medical bills."

"Just make sure my family gets something," he said. "Don't you ever relax?" Even at midnight in Ocean City NJ, standing before the majesty of the Atlantic Ocean, the attorney still dressed to the nines in a three-piece suit, always at the command of his duty and profession. "Have a drink?"

"I never drink on duty," the lawyer said.

"You deserve it, Mr. Marino," Oliver said then sipped. "You've given me back my night."

"A night's not very much," he said.

"It can last forever, and after nearly losing it, I'll always savor it."

"You're a brave man."

"No, I'm not," Oliver said. "It's not like the movies. I'm terrified, and all I can do is distract myself from it, focus on the daily minutia."

"Well, I hope my condo distracts well," the lawyer said.

"It's very gracious of you."

"Though I know it's not what you expected," the lawyer said, looking through the patio door at the collapsed wheelchair leaning against the living room wall. "You didn't fail."

Oliver gripped the foam handle of his cane. "It took me nearly all my life to learn that it isn't always failure when things don't turn out the way you planned."

"This is true."

"You know, this would make a good story," he said, taking out his little notebook; however, instead of writing it down, he started to laugh then tossed his unsatisfied journal off the condo's patio into the darkness. "I just wish Jackie was here with us now."

They both sat in silence, contemplating the dark dark horizon hovering over the Atlantic.

"Father, Son and holy shit!" Jackie said as she shut the sliding door behind her then limped over to them, leaning on her cane, still not steady on her new prosthetic leg.

"You're wearing sunglasses at night?" Oliver asked.

She ignored him then collapsed into the chair. Skin clung to her bones, and he watched her face grimace, her mouth randomly tense as she endured sudden and intense bouts of pain, pain no longer mollified by opiates. When CNN had run his story, faceless donations poured in to their lives, and the new prosthetic, the palliative hospice care she could now afford had for a time improved both her spirits and quality of life, but eventually the gains faded and medicines delivered diminishing returns. "You're a good man, Mikey," she said to the attorney. "And you were a good friend to my husband—may he rot in jail. I signed the papers and left them on your desk."

He leaned down and kissed her on the cheek. "What's your plans?"

"I want to stay," she said. "For the night." She carried a thermos of coffee she'd freshly brewed to keep them alert till sunrise.

"You and your friend enjoy the condo for as long as you want," he said. "Mary took the kids to Florida anyway, and I'm not a big fan of sand in my shoes." He did a partial bow then closed the patio door behind him.

"Do you want a drink?" Oliver asked.

"I don't want it to become a habit," she said, and they both snickered. "This thing itches."

"Just relax and enjoy the beach. It's not Alaska, but the night is young and its ours." He got up, lit the fire pit on the patio. When he returned to her side, Jackie took his hand.

"One more night," she said then took out a bottle, swallowed a pill and shook the cylinder like a rattle.

"Can't you smile for me?"

"At sunrise, I'm leaving," she said, and she didn't smile. He knew it wasn't her.

"*Quel dommage,*" he said then put his finger to her lips.

Some Kind of Friend

Inspired by *Some Kind of Friend* from the album
Here Comes the Night (1982)

Christine Verstraete

The young woman stood on the front stoop, patiently waiting for me to invite her in.

"Thanks for letting me come talk to you," she said, her smile bright. "I only need about twenty minutes, if you don't mind?"

Her name eluded me for a moment. Lisa, that's what it was; Lisa Lane, a reporter from the local newspaper.

She must've sensed my apprehension and repeated her promise. "I won't take up too much of your time. Honest."

Thus far, every interview request I'd received had been turned down, from newspapers to TV stations, both local and national. But, since she was here, I changed my mind. "Very well, come in."

She followed me in to a large living room I'd decorated in gold and white, the walls covered with gilded picture frames of my much younger self and other former Copacabana dancers dressed in Brazilian-inspired costumes. Black-and-white images of old New York lined the white marble fireplace mantel.

With the recent anniversary of the closing of the famous nightclub, and my 100th birthday right around the corner, I must've been feeling sentimental to let this reporter come to my home.

The young woman seated herself on the white couch across from me, setting up her camera and opening a notebook. I tamped down the butterflies in my stomach, poured some lemonade, and passed her the filled glass.

"I never give interviews, you know."

"I know, and I really appreciate it," she responded, sipping her drink. "I'm glad you did. Mmm, this is good. People often forget trailblazers like you."

"Thank you for that. We were the 'It Girls' in our day, you know. But there was a lot of darkness behind the sequins, too."

Her smile and friendly manner put me at ease as she began her questions.

"If you don't mind, I'll record this, too."

I nodded and stared at my wrinkled hands. The sequined costumes had been replaced long ago by a cashmere sweater and plain brown pants, but even if I'd changed outwardly, I remained in good shape with some calisthenics and Pilates. That had helped me maintain the graceful lines and form that had made me a star in the dance line of the old Copacabana nightclub in the Forties.

"When was the last time you saw anyone from the Copa?"

Despite agreeing to this, it still bothered me having to relive parts of the past. I knew where she was going in her line of questioning and that it couldn't be avoided. A deep breath helped calm me before answering.

"Thirty years it's been, but it felt like yesterday. I saw Mina at a café for but a moment. Our eyes met, but she quickly glanced away."

My mind went back over the decades, remembering my fellow dancer and sometime friend, Mina Ruiz.

I gazed out the window, my blue eyes still observant if dim with age, my smile wistful as the memories unfolded.

Some things I tend to forget, but those days came to me as if they'd happened yesterday—the excitement and drama and prestige of dancing in the front line, the crowds drinking and laughing, the admirers who left flowers and knocked on my dressing room door hoping I'd join them for an after-show drink and some company. I could still see the smoke and smell the cloying aroma of the cigarettes, and the scent of Chanel No. 5 and Sandalwood floating in the air.

"She'd been a friend, a good friend, or so I'd thought."

"Until she betrayed you?"

I dared not answer.

* * *

My thoughts went back to that first meeting. The past unfolded and enveloped me again like an old friend.

I'd boarded a bus, fresh from my parent's farm in the Midwest and eager to make my dreams of becoming a singer or dancer come true. Despite war raging across Europe and fears of America's involvement, I had one destination in mind: the famed Copacabana nightclub in New York, the place where the famous—and the infamous—hung out and performed.

Lucky for me, a dancer was sick so I got to the chance to fill in at the club. I'd been practicing my steps and stretching my legs when she came in. Mina was beautiful, breathtakingly so, a sultry blonde bombshell with a curvaceous figure that I knew would steal all the attention once she got on stage. She'd sidled next to me, her friendliness nevertheless putting me at ease.

"Hi, I'm Mina. They said I should warm up first. You been working here long?"

I laughed at the question. "I've only been here a couple weeks. I'm just a fill-in, but I hope they'll have more openings soon."

"Oh, me, too. I want to dance in the front line! Wouldn't that be fun?"

Her enthusiasm was contagious. I wanted that, too, hoping it wouldn't take long to work up to regular hours as a second-tier dancer and eventually have the chance to move up to the front. That's where the money was. You got noticed there. The front-line girls got a lot of perks, extra tips, some were even invited to show and movie auditions by local directors.

I'd also learned pretty fast that it was best to stay away from certain people, like the shadowy men dressed in their flashy, expensive suits. I hadn't realized until later that the mobster Frank Costello was initially a part owner of the club, and he had his hired muscle there to keep an eye on things. A couple of them were supposed to help keep the girls safe from too-pushy men in the audience, but it was soon obvious no one was there to keep us safe from them, either.

That didn't bother Mina. She flirted with everyone, and didn't hesitate to give an encouraging smile to one of the regular goons sitting at the bar.

I lowered my voice.

"Mina, I wouldn't encourage them. Don't you know who they are?"

She shrugged. "I don't care. I don't want to be dancing in the back line forever. He's got connections. Besides, he's rather good-looking, don't you think?"

I held back a grimace, not fond of his sly ways and oily looks.

The reporter cleared her throat, pulling me out of the past. "Mina didn't listen to your warning?"

"Mina wouldn't listen to anybody," I answered. "More lemonade?"

The reporter waved her hand no and urged me to continue.

"She was right in a way," I explained. "Once she got involved with Johnny, she moved up fast, from fill-in, to second line, and then to the front line. I was right behind her, but I put in a lot of extra hours of practice to do it while Mina was out after work nightclubbing until the wee hours. I know she put in a good word for me, but I told her not to. I didn't like Johnny and how he treated her, and I couldn't stand how he tried to make time with all the girls."

* * *

I remembered one particular day when I'd come in to get ready for the night's shows. Mina had arrived before anyone else. She sat at the dressing table patting on extra foundation and powder in an attempt to cover the bruises on her face.

"It's nothing," she said. "I drank too much and fell. I'll be fine."

The reporter brought me back to the present. "Was Mina fine?"

"She said she was, but I saw the flicker of fear on her face before she hid it. I told her I'd help her get away from him, that she didn't have to be afraid."

"What did she say?"

"She told me I was a nosy jealous bitch and to mind my own

business. Bet you won't print that."

The reporter only smiled.

* * *

"Why did you leave the Copa after only six months?" the reporter asked.

I sighed, not at all happy to be reminded again of how my dreams had faded and tarnished.

"The club was having lots of problems," I recalled. "Those mob guys were getting too bold. They wouldn't leave me or the other girls alone. As much as I loved the job, it was time to move on. I found another job dancing at a smaller place out by the harbor. It wasn't as prestigious, but it had decent musicians and was drawing the crowds. It seemed like a good move."

"But it wasn't," the reporter prompted, breaking into my musing.

"It was, for a while… and then Mina showed up. She was trying to get away from Johnny, she said. But it didn't work."

The reporter pulled out a news clipping from her notebook. "Here's what Louella Parsons said in her column of January 21, 1941."

> A certain dancer, Clarissa Simone, was questioned by police recently for the death of reputed mobster Johnny DiStefenato, who was found shot dead last week in the back room of the small nightclub, The Bar by the Harbor. Police also questioned her former friend and fellow dancer Mina Ruiz, who had worked with Simone at the famous Copacabana, and who was romantically linked with DiStefenato. Was it really a lover's spat gone wrong, or does the sultry dancer Simone have more to do with the death than she's telling? We'll be sharing updates on this juicy report in coming days.

I couldn't hold back my snort of contempt. "Nothing could be further from the truth. One thing I did learn early on was to keep out of the reach of Louella. Once she got her claws in you, her fingernails weren't the only things dripping red."

"Why didn't you try to clear up the rumors then?" Lane asked, tapping the pen on her notepad. "You never publicly commented on the case, even when you were called in for questioning by the police."

"What could I say?" I responded, my anguish growing. "When Johnny showed up at the bar, Mina finally gave in and began going out with him again. Then I saw the bruises and knew he was back to slapping her around. I told the bar owners what he was doing and asked them to keep him out, but they ignored me. He was a big customer, flashed a lot of money about."

"Mina said you were jealous and involved with him behind her back, so you shot him. Was that what happened?"

* * *

It had been a long night, I remembered. The place had closed in the wee hours, everyone gone except for the owner hiding out in his back office counting the night's proceeds. I'd changed and was ready to leave when the dressing room door opened and in walked a most unwelcome visitor.

Johnny stood in the doorway, a toothpick hanging from the corner of his mouth, his beady eyes scanning me up and down like meat hanging on a rack. I'd jumped to my feet, hurriedly easing open the drawer on my dressing table where I kept a small pistol as he slinked his way into the room.

"So, doll, looks like you and me got some unfinished bizness."

He unbuttoned his coat and threw it aside, then proceeded to undo his belt. I gulped, trying to keep some distance between us.

"Look, Johnny, we're not alone. The owner's here. Leave me be or I'll scream."

My threats only made him laugh. "You think he's gonna save you? I told him me and you had some things to talk about. He said I should lock up when I'm done."

He lunged before I could grab the pistol, wrapping his beefy arms around me. I fought him off as he pawed at me and pressed his ugly lips against my neck, but it was like trying to free myself of a boa constrictor. I pushed back a wave of fear and nausea as he tore my blouse and pulled at my skirt. He fumbled with my clothes while I struggled to get away from him when a familiar voice stopped him better than any of my attempts.

I stared, shocked to see Mina standing by the door—a blunt-nosed revolver in her hand and pointed our way.

"I said you were gonna pay for what you did to me," she warned, cocking the revolver. "I'd get you, too, Clarissa, for cheating with him behind my back, but he's more to blame. Let her go."

"Listen, doll face, it's not what you think," he plead, knowing when to cut his losses, it seemed.

"I'm not listening to you anymore, Johnny. It's all that and more. Clarissa, get over here." She waved the gun at him, and then at me. "Now."

I took the moment to free myself from his grasp and rushed behind her.

"Listen, you better hand over that little pistol right now," Johnny warned, moving closer.

"Or what, huh? What're you going to do, Johnny, beat me again?"

He ignored her and growled, taking another step toward her when… BLAM!

As if in slow motion, I watched him grab his chest and slump to the floor, a pool of blood spreading across the front of his custom-made white shirt.

"Mina, no! What did you do?"

The silence grew deafening as I slowly eased the gun from her and dropped it in my bag. My mind racing, I grabbed an old shirt, wiping down the sides of the door and anywhere else she'd touched, before yanking her into the hall.

"Mina, c'mon, we have to get out of here."

Finally, she came to her senses and pulled away from me. "Leave me alone. This is all your fault. None of this would've happened if not for you. I'm going home. Try and stop me."

"The police'll be looking for you. Everyone knows about you and

Johnny."

She glared at me, her eyes cold and as hard as diamonds. "So? Let them come. Like I said, it's all your fault and I'll tell them that. I didn't do anything, did I?"

She had a point, and I knew it. I'd pulled her out of there and taken the gun. I was just as guilty as she was.

* * *

"That was the last time I saw her," I mumbled, remembering the reporter sitting there.

"Where?" she asked, not sure what I meant.

"At the bar, after Johnny was shot."

"So, she did shoot him?"

I didn't answer, all my strength gone, the memories simply too much to bear.

"I'm sorry. I-I'm very tired. We'll have to end this now. I'm going to lie down. Please let yourself out and lock the door behind you."

She said her thanks, gathered her belongings, and left, leaving me to reflect again on things I didn't want to remember… memories I thought I'd left behind decades ago.

My memory had become foggier in recent months, some events fading into others, but I often got a funny feeling when something wasn't quite right, like this time. I just didn't know what it was.

* * *

Her story and interview with Clarissa had turned out well, but Lane regretted that it had been mostly overlooked and buried in the back of the paper after the arrest of a big public figure. A sense of sadness filled her when she saw the obituary in the paper two days later:

Noted Dancer Dead

Clarisa Simone, former dancer of the famed Copacabana Club and the Bar at the Harbor in the 1940s, died yesterday of natural causes. She had just turned 100. Simone and fellow dancer, the late Mina Ruiz, had been linked to the 1941 murder of mobster Johnny DiStefenato, but no one was ever

formerly charged with the shooting.

* * *

Lane was surprised to receive a letter shortly after from a local attorney whose ads she'd seen on late night TV. She quickly read it, then made the call.

After picking up the box at the lawyer's office, she took it home, wondering what the octogenarian had bequeathed to her. Even if the dancer had no remaining family, Lane thought it odd to receive anything considering they'd only met once.

Opening the box, she found a signed, framed photo of Clarissa on top of several books. Lane realized how fortunate she'd been to get the last interview with the former dancer and appreciated the gesture. She set the frame on the coffee table and turned to the books.

Most of the volumes were well-known tomes of the 1940s—Ernest Hemingway's *For Whom the Bell Tolls*, *A Tree Grows in Brooklyn* by Betty Smith, Shirley Jackson's *The Lottery and Other Stories*, plus a few mystery novels. She flipped to the copyright pages, noticing a couple were first editions. Hmm, might be worth something.

The last book in the box had a note taped on the cover. In spidery handwriting, the dancer had written, *For Lisa.*

Even more curious now, Lane eyed the book, not recognizing the author or the title. Why did Clarissa tag this one?

She flipped the first few pages, but nothing else had been written inside. Figuring it for a nice memento, she moved to set the book aside when she noticed it felt heavier than the others. Puzzled, she re-opened the book, her pulse racing when she saw that some of the pages had been stuck together.

She turned to the back section and gasped, stunned to find a hole carved into the center of the book. And in it sat a small black revolver— the gun that must've been used in the DiStefenato murder and had never been found.

But why in the world did Clarissa have it? Why had she saved it? More importantly, why had she given it to her?

Lane knew turning the weapon over to the authorities could make her career. Making this public also meant tarnishing the memory of a woman who not only hadn't admitted to any wrong-doing, but had been cleared by police of the crime.

She stared at the gun, questioning her own motives.

After several minutes, Lane closed the book and removed the note. The boxed books went in the back of her closet until she decided what to do with them, and especially how to best dispose of the gun.

Maybe she could donate the whole box anonymously to the library or take it to a thrift store.

A better idea came to mind.

She went outside and stood in the backyard. This would be a good day to get some planting done for the sweet older lady she rented her apartment from. The bright reds and purples of the flowers already in bloom brightened the yard. The sweet scent of the yellow and red rosebushes waiting to be planted filled the air.

Remembering the brightly colored costumes and floral headpieces that Clarissa and the other performers had worn, Lane decided this was a more appropriate way to remember the former dancer and keep her decades-old secret.

She got to work.

Digging the hole a bit deeper, she dropped the gun in before covering it with some dirt, setting in the rosebush, and finally adding more dirt on top.

Once finished, she stood back and admired her handiwork with a smile. She thought Clarissa would approve.

Getting Even Now

Inspired by *Even Now* from the album
Even Now (1978)
Shari Held

February 2024

Eight o'clock at night. I'd spent thirteen hours at the office negotiating real estate deals, consulting with lawyers to see how far the company could go and remain legit, and strategizing novel ways to stiff the competition. I was good at my job. More than good. But I was bone-tired as I climbed the stairs to our bedroom. Nothing new. I'd learned to live with it over the last year since I became the president and CEO of L. Bolton & Associates.

"Edward, you're home at last." Jacquelin gave me a hug. "And not a moment too soon. We're due at the museum benefit by nine."

"Sorry. I didn't forget, but my meeting ran longer than I anticipated."

Jacquelin was nothing short of perfection in a simple, figure-hugging black velvet gown, every strand of her blond hair in place. She wore shimmering diamond earrings and a gold necklace with an impressive diamond pendant nested in her cleavage—a gift from her father, chairman of the board and my boss.

"No problem. It will only take me a minute."

As always, she'd laid everything I needed on my side of the bed, from my tuxedo to the diamond and onyx cufflinks she'd given me as a wedding present. When I finished dressing, Jacquelin gave me an air kiss, so she wouldn't smudge her freshly applied lipstick, and we were off.

She'd hired a limo to deliver us to the museum. Jaquelin didn't bombard me with talk about her charity work during the ride, allowing me time to unwind before we arrived. Usually, I poured a scotch and decompressed. But not tonight.

All I could think of was you, Marilyn, my first and only true love. The way your auburn hair sprawled across your pillow as you waited for me in our bed. The way our bodies fit together as if they were custom-made for one another. And your expressive eyes, that could glow with childlike wonder one minute and burn with desire the next. It's been three years, but I think of you all the time and I miss you every day.

I wish I could confide in Jacquelin the way I used to confide in you, but I don't dare.

I shouldn't complain. By all appearances, I've got it made. I live in an upscale mansion in a gated community in Carmel. Not Carmel by the Sea, but Carmel, Indiana, one of the highest rated cities in which to live. We belong to an exclusive country club, dine in swank restaurants and vacation in Europe or island paradises. Jacquelin is easy-going, gorgeous, talented, and a gracious hostess. We Clarks live a luxurious existence.

If I had never met you, Marilyn, I might have been fine with my current lifestyle. But I still long for parts of the life I once had with you. How I'd love to rid myself of my monkey suits and work at a regular job where I could clock out at five and come home to you. I'd change into a well-worn pair of Levis and a leather jacket with studs, and we'd hop on our Harley and head to our favorite pub and shoot pool. Other nights, I'd go solo, order a pitcher of beer at the pub, watch a sports game, and enjoy some guy talk. "How about those Boilermakers?" "What about that hot babe on the latest TV show?"

But those days are long gone since my father-in-law, Larry, changed my path in life. And there's no turning back. I suppose I should be grateful to him. After all, he's the reason I'm head of one of the largest commercial real estate companies in North America. But I'll always wonder, if I had turned Larry down and left the company, would you and I still be together?

* * *

Three Years Earlier

The company's head honcho, Larry Bolton, had asked to meet with me after hours. I'd been trying to figure out why all day since I received his message. I came up with zip. I knocked on his office door—not too soft; not too forceful.

"Come in."

I opened the door and shut it behind me. Another man was in the room with Larry.

"Edward, this is Fleenor. He conducts research for me. Feels out how receptive people might be to our offers." Larry chuckled like it was a secret joke between them.

Fleenor glanced in my direction but didn't smile or extend his hand.

Larry turned toward Fleenor and said, "I need that deal closed ASAP. Do whatever it takes."

Fleenor, apparently a man of few words, nodded, then strode out the door and left us.

Larry sat in his oversize, cushy leather chair and puffed on a Cuban cigar. "Sit down," he said, indicating the chair in front of his desk. "Cigar?"

"Yes, sir."

Larry handed me a cigar and moved the lighter closer to me. I hoped I wouldn't embarrass myself as I lit it. I wasn't offered such a classy smoke every day. "Thank you."

"You're probably wondering why I called you here after hours and told you not to mention it to anyone."

"Yes, sir. I figured it was something really good or very bad."

Larry chuckled. "Well, boy, and drop the 'sir' stuff, I think you'll consider this in the 'really good' category. You remind me a lot of myself when I was young. I worked my way through college, too. Took me six years to graduate with a BS. You earned your MBA in four, is that right?"

"Yes." *So far, so good.*

I've heard good things about you. You've got street smarts as well as book learning. It takes both, these days. If you had to describe yourself in three words, what would they be?"

I pretended to give it some thought, then answered with what I was sure he wanted to hear. "I'm hungry, assertive, and loyal."

"Good. Any history of drugs, excessive drinking, or a criminal record I should know about? Best not lie to me, son. I'm no sentimental fool. I'll have Fleenor check you out. I don't like surprises."

"No, sir. No problems with any of those."

Larry didn't say anything immediately, just bored holes into me with his eyes while he sucked on his cigar. I puffed on mine, hoping I looked like the kind of man he wanted for the job, or wherever this was going.

Finally, he dropped his bomb. "How much would you like to be my successor?

I leaned forward in my chair. It tipped precariously toward the desk, but I managed to right it. "Me? But, what about Simmonds and Mullins? I thought they were the top contenders."

"They think so, too, the entitled little kiss-ass sycophants. Harvard grads are a dime a dozen. Of course, if you aren't interested. . ."

"You bet I'm interested. But, why me?"

"I want someone who will follow in my path, make decisions the way I would make them. Someone who can wheel and deal and close the job to my satisfaction. I think you're my man. Most importantly, I want to keep the company in the family."

I shook my head. "What? But I'm not family."

"You will be when you marry my daughter."

"Marry? But I've got a girlfriend."

"You want to become my second-in-command? Become respected? Have people look up to you instead of turning down their noses at the kid from the slums?"

"Yes, but—"

"Break up with her."

"But I love Marilyn. I can't—"

Larry banged his fist on his desk. His cigar dropped to the floor, scattering ash on the Persian carpet. "You can and you will if you want to be this company's next CEO.

What's it going to be?"

* * *

May 2024

Accepting Larry's offer was the hardest thing I've ever done. I would have been giddy with joy if the job hadn't come with conditions. Leaving you, Marilyn, tore my gut to shreds. Didn't stop me from doing it, though. I rationalized. Chances are we'd break up anyway. I was just speeding up the inevitable.

Larry had made it clear that if I refused there was no place for me in the company.

I might never get another opportunity like this.

I took the coward's way out. Every time I think of how you must have felt when you read my note, I cringe with shame. Larry gave me the keys to one of the company's guest suites, and I moved into another world—new suits, shiny Mercedes, a company credit card. I was dazzled. The whirlwind activity surrounding my new position was fun initially. And I must admit, I got a kick out of seeing the expression on Simmonds's and Mullins's faces when Larry promoted me to Senior VP.

Honestly, it was like I was born to the job. I loved the challenge of devising winning strategies. With Larry's tutelage, I honed those skills. Jaquelin and I became engaged. Me, a kid from the wrong side of town, with a wife who had attended the Sorbonne. What a hoot.

But Larry began asking me to do things I didn't feel comfortable doing, like making changes to documentation without proper paperwork. I'd heard rumors he'd pulled off shady deals before. Then I overheard him threaten one of our clients. I enjoyed a challenge, but I liked beating people with my brain, not hired brawn. Everyone I knew was beholden to or involved with Larry. I didn't have anyone I could trust. Especially my own wife.

It was you I needed, Marilyn. I yearned for your touch, to lie in bed and talk for hours, revealing my insecurities, my secrets. With you, I could be myself with no fear of judgment or ridicule. I didn't have to be Mr. Perfect.

One night, when Jacquelin was visiting her sister in San Fran for a couple weeks, I couldn't help myself. I cruised past our old apartment and parked across the street. Then, like an answer to my prayers, you walked out the door. The streetlight shone on your face, and I saw your lovely auburn hair cascading down your back. Before I knew what I was doing, I jumped from the car and ran to you.

I was thrilled you took me back after I'd treated you shabbily. I spent every night Jacquelin was gone with you. When we were in bed, I told you all the things I couldn't confess to Jaquelin. I wasn't sure whose side she would be on. Mine or her father's. With you, I was free to reveal Larry's dirty little secrets. I enjoyed the challenge of bending the law, but he broke it. And now, he was getting me mixed up in his schemes.

The last night I saw you, you suggested I gather any evidence against Larry and place it somewhere safe. I headed back to the office to see what I could find, promising to stop by in a couple days.

I disabled the office cameras and unlocked Larry's office door—talents I'd learned in "the hood" and at a security job I'd worked while going to school. I checked Larry's computer first. Larry was proficient in many areas, but computer skills, not so much. I'd learned his password because he'd left it lying on his desk. It was the surname of a former president and businessman Larry idolized and the year Larry had founded the company.

I copied recordings of meetings and documentation that offered proof of some of Larry's shady deals on a flash drive. I also found folders on me, Mullins, Simmonds, and Fleenor. I glanced through them. No surprise. They contained blackmail fodder against all four of us. I deleted the contents of those folders and emptied his trash. I knew Larry didn't trust the cloud, so I jimmied the lock on his file cabinet and pulled the corresponding folders.

I stashed everything in a safety deposit box I opened in a different bank than the one I normally used.

I couldn't get away to see you for a week. When I did, you were gone. Your apartment empty. I called your cell phone, but there was no answer.

Marilyn, where are you? What made you leave? What will I do without you?

* * *

Three Weeks Later

I've still heard nothing from you, Marilyn. Today, I'm going to confront Larry. Ask him if he knows something about your disappearance. He'll tell me where you are, or I'll threaten him with the evidence I found.

When I told Larry I wanted to meet, he suggested his office. As chairman of the board, he kept his office, the best one in the building, although he doesn't come in on any set schedule. He looked composed although I suspect he knew what was coming. He folded up the latest issue of *The Wall Street Journal* and lit a cigar. He didn't offer me one.

"So, what's on your mind, son?" he asked, his voice frosty.

I gulped, then got straight to the point. "Marilyn's gone. What have you done with her?

Larry didn't look surprised. His cold eyes glared at me. "The question, *son*, is what have *you* done?" He steepled his hands on his desk. "Let me see. You broke your wedding vows to my daughter, for one thing. You hightailed it over to Marilyn's place every chance you got while Jacquelin was gone. I could forgive you for that. But I can't forgive you for breaking your vow of secrecy to me. You told that little slut about our business deals."

I could feel my face flush. "You had me tailed?

Larry's smile told me all I wanted to know.

I didn't know if I was angrier that he called Marilyn a "slut" or that he'd had me followed. "I never—"

"Save it. You did. I have proof." Larry punched a few buttons on his keyboard and Marilyn's voice filled the room. "Please. Eddie didn't tell me anything. I don't know what you're talking about. You've got to believe me."

Larry paused the recording. He must have practiced his computer moves all afternoon. He smiled an evil smile. "Want to hear the rest of the recording? The part where she gives you up?"

My hands gripped the chair arms. "You son of a bitch. Marilyn's harmless. She wouldn't know who to tell. What did you do? Pay her off with a bundle of money and relocate her? Make her promise not to see me again?"

Larry shrugged his shoulders. "You have only yourself to blame. Return everything you stole from my office, and I'll consider telling you where she is. Understand?

Now get out of my sight."

* * *

I made a quick stop at my safety deposit box, then went to a nearby coffee shop. I was positive my office was bugged, and I didn't want Larry to hear this conversation. I called Fleenor, my father-in-law's fixer, and asked him to meet me there. Then I ordered a carafe of coffee and two mugs.

Fleenor showed up and sat down. His face was one big question mark. I'd never contacted him before.

I poured coffee, then threw a folder on the table between us.

"What's this?" Fleenor asked.

"Open it."

As he read, his eyes narrowed. His fists clenched. He kept reading for a few minutes, then closed the folder. "Where did you get this?"

"Where do you think?"

He drummed his hand on the table. "Why are you showing me this?"

I leaned forward and looked him straight in the eyes. "Because I believe you have information I need about a certain Marilyn Gold. Am

I right?" I paused. "I want to know where she is. In return, the folder is yours to keep."

"Are you sure you have everything?"

I shrugged. "I deleted the info on his computer and from his file cabinet. He may have other copies, but even if he does, you'll know what proof he has on you, so you can cover your tracks. That ought to be worth something."

Turned out it was. Fleenor pulled a moleskin notebook from his pocket, wrote down an address, tore the sheet out, and laid it on the table in front of me. He stood, took the folder, and left.

I had one more person to confront, and she would be the hardest one of all.

* * *

I arrived home within minutes. Jacquelin greeted me at the door, wearing slim black capris and an oversized white linen shirt, her hair in gold ringlets around her heart-shaped face. "Hi, Hon. This is a nice surprise. I'll make a pitcher of martinis and let's sit on the deck."

"Sure. I'll change while you're doing that."

When I joined her on the deck, she handed me a martini and leaned toward me for a kiss. She wore Joy perfume, a sweet, floral scent that matched her demeanor.

I hated myself for what I was going to say. But I was going to come clean. "Thank you, I can use that."

I gulped my martini, then turned toward her, expression as solemn as if I were in the front pew during a funeral service, and said, "Hon, we need to talk."

"That doesn't sound good." She refreshed our drinks. Her hand trembled as she poured another round of martinis.

"Did you truly love me when you accepted my proposal? Or did you do it to please your father?"

She dropped her eyes to the container of rosemary, geraniums, and sweet potato vine near her feet. "I. . ."

"Be truthful. That's all I ask."

"Okay, but I don't want to hurt you, Edward. I liked you, of course, but I married you because Daddy told me I had to. To keep the company in the family."

I took another swig of my martini. "That's what I thought. Is there someone else you wanted to marry?"

Red blotches appeared on Jacquelin's creamy skin. "Yes, there was someone. But I was always faithful to you. I would never have embarrassed you."

"I know. There was once someone else for me, too. Someone I loved very much. Someone your father made me give up."

"I guess my father screwed us both, didn't he?"

"Yes, he did."

"Why are you telling me this now, Edward? Has something happened?"

"Yes. And I'm sorry about this. But I reconnected with Marilyn while you were visiting your sister. I made the mistake of telling her about some of your father's deals. I didn't know Fleenor was tailing me. He evidently bugged her place and taped our conversations during that time. Your father bribed her and relocated her so I couldn't find her."

Jacquelin straightened herself upright and fixed her gaze on him. "I believe it. Daddy threatened to spread terrible career-ruining rumors about Ted if I ever contacted him again. But what could I do? What can you do? Daddy controls everything."

"We'll see about that," I said.

* * *

One Month Later

I'd reconnected with Marilyn who had agreed to take me back. Now, there would be no more wondering where she was. She would be by my side, right where she belonged. I'm not sure what I'll end up doing, We can live on Marilyn's hush money and the money I received for selling my company stock for a long time.

I'd advised Jacquelin and Alice, her mother, to do the same. I was no longer with the company, so no one would think twice about my dumping the stock. Jacquelin and Alice could claim they had sold their stock because of the headlines in the newspapers and rags about Larry's many affairs. Fleenor had been so pissed off by the folder Larry had compiled on him, he willingly revealed the names of all Larry's women to help Alice. Larry had evidently promised a lot of them things he never delivered on, and they were plenty willing to spill their guts to the media.

Alice promptly filed for divorce. I gave her a copy of incriminating documentation on Larry for her to use as leverage if he tried to cheat her out of the house and her share of their cash.

Jacquelin was now engaged to Ted, and they planned to wed as soon as possible.

Today, Leah, my former administrative assistant and ally, informed me that Larry and the executive staff had left for a retreat earlier this morning and now would be a good time to collect my belongings.

I stood in my old office and surveyed everything—from the plush carpet, to the mahogany desk, to the tasteful artwork hanging on the walls, to the scenic view of the city from the window. I'd probably never have an office as luxurious as this again, but I didn't care. If dishonesty is required to get ahead in the corporate world, I wanted no part of it.

Now, I have one last thing to do. I placed a copy of Simmonds's folder and the dirt on Larry in a manilla envelope addressed to Mullins and a copy of Mullins's folder and Larry's info in a manilla envelope addressed to Simmonds, marked them "Personal" in red, sealed them, and gave them to Leah with instructions to deliver them directly into their hands.

Then I picked up my hat, shut off the lights, grabbed the box of my belongings, and headed toward the elevator.

May the best man win.

The Literary Fanilows

Karen Keeley first fell in love with a good who-done-it when she stumbled upon Rex Stout and his *Nero Wolfe* novels at a used bookstore in northwestern Ontario, what she lovingly calls her Archie books. She is the author of "Sticks and Stones, three murder mysteries," and; "There Goes the Neighbourhood, Syd Malloy, Private Investigator, short stories." Her short fiction has appeared in anthologies published by Sisters in Crime—Canada West; Celestial Echo Press; Gutter Books; Outcast Press; Last Waltz Publishing; Black Beacon Books; and many others. A proud Canuck living north of the 49th parallel, she divides her time between family, friends, the outdoors, and writing—not necessarily in that order.

Linda Kay Hardie is a freelance writer in Reno, Nevada. She writes short stories in many genres including horror, dark fantasy, and crime, but not romance. She tried once, and everyone ended up dead. Tragic. She also writes recipes and is the reigning Spam champion for Nevada (yes, the tasty treat canned mystery meat). Her writing has won awards dating back to fifth grade, with first place for an essay on fire safety. In 2022, she was honored with the Sierra Arts Foundation Literary Arts Award for fiction. For more, see
https://www.amazon.com/author/lindakayhardie

Adam Gorgoni was born and raised in New York City and is a graduate of Harvard University where he studied Latin American History and US Foreign Policy. He makes his home in Los Angeles where, when he is not on the tennis court, he is a professional music composer and producer. His film scoring credits include Sundance favorite *Starting Out In The Evening*, Deauville Grand Prize winner *The Dead Girl*, and cult comedy classic *Waiting*. Television work: USA Network's *Necessary Roughness*, the CW series *Aliens In America*, Lorne Michaels' ABC comedy *Sons and Daughters*, as well as shows for NBC, HBO, Discovery Channel, Bravo, and National Geographic. Adam has extensive experience in music for advertising, with clients such as Toyota, AT&T, IBM, and Mastercard. He served as a co-producer of the ground breaking musical *Head Over Heels*, which debuted on Broadway in 2018.

In recent years (i.e. the pandemic) he has returned to an old love, crime fiction, and previously appeared in the White City Press anthology *(I Just) Died In Your Arms: Crime Fiction Inspired by One-Hit Wonders*.

Maya St. Clair is a writer/editor from Mundelein, Illinois, whose work blends horror, fantasy, and history. In college, she studied Renaissance literature and history; afterwards, she worked at *Heavy Metal* magazine, and is currently a staff contributor at *Radon, Locus,* and others.

Matt McGee is a six-time Pushcart nominee working in the Los Angeles area. He was born in Upstate NY at a time when music came in two forms: a General Electric radio atop the family refrigerator and Columbia House cassettes, both of which were controlled by his mother, who also harbored a *Manilow Live!* poster inside a kitchen cabinet. His collections *Diversions* and *Leaving Rayette* are available on Amazon.

Laurie Stevens is the author of the Gabriel McRay thriller series. The books have won thirteen awards, including Kirkus Review's "Best of" and a Random House Editors' Book of the Month. International Thriller Writers says she's "cracked the code" regarding writing psychological suspense, while Suspense Magazine claims she's the "leader of the pack." Laurie's short stories have appeared in anthologies and magazines, and she co-edited the 2019 Los Angeles Sisters in Crime anthology *Fatally Haunted*. Her newest novel, *The Return*, is a sci-fi fantasy that pits artificial intelligence against human consciousness. Laurie slipped into comfortable shoes and returned to writing dark, psychological suspense with her contribution to *A Killing at the Copa*. An active member of Mystery Writers of America, International Thriller Writers, Science Fiction Writers of America, and Sisters in Crime, Laurie lives in the hills outside of Los Angeles with her husband, two snakes, and a handsome white cat.

Caleb Weinhardt (he/him) is a queer and trans writer from the Pacific Northwest. When he's not writing stories, he enjoys hiking with his dog, Winnie, and making music. His work appears in or is forthcoming in *tiny frights*, *Major 7th Magazine*, *Punk Noir*, *Blanket Gravity*, and *Cosmorama*. Find him at calebweinhardt.com and on Twitter at @PNWcaleb.

Kurtis Rupé survived a career in the insurance industry and is now happily unemployed, embracing a new chapter in his life. Before moving with his partner and three dogs to Tucson, Arizona, he spent most of his life near the coast in Long Beach, Orange County, and the San Francisco Bay Area of California. His poetry has been featured in publications such as Chiron Review, Nerve Cowboy, and Pearl, and he recently won second place in a local limerick competition. Beyond writing, Kurtis takes history, political science, and literature classes, attends the Tucson Festival of Books each year, and enjoys Tai Chi, hiking in the mountains, and volunteering at his local Friends of the Library bookstore.

Recita Clemons was born in a town so small she refers to her birthplace as, Vermillion Parish, Louisiana. She traveled frequently as an Air Force brat before the family settled in Denver, Colorado. After high school, she graduated from Howard University in Washington, D.C., with a Journalism degree.
After several years writing articles and manuals for a telecommunications company, she began writing novels in 2015 under

R. Lanier Clemons, featuring Private Investigator Jonelle Sweet. The second novel in the series, *Gone Missing*, won the African American category of the Next Generation Indie Book Awards and the third novel, *The Trickster*, was a finalist in the National Indie Excellence Awards. She lives in Maryland with diva cat Lucy and feisty pony Ramsey. Recita is a member of Sisters in Crime, Crime Writers of Color and the Maryland Writers Association.

J. M. Taylor spins his sinister fantasies in Boston where he lives with his wife and son. He has appeared in *Tough, Wildside Black Cat,* and *AHMM,* among others. He also had a story in (*I Just) Died in Your Arms* from White City Press. His books include *Night of the Furies,* from New Pulp Press, *Dark Heat,* from Genretarium, and *No Score* from Unnerving. When he's not writing, he teaches under an assumed name. You can find him at jmtaylorcrimewriter.com and on Facebook at *Night of the Furies.*

John M. Floyd is the author of more than a thousand short stories in publications like *Alfred Hitchcock's Mystery Magazine, Ellery Queen's Mystery Magazine, Strand Magazine,* Woman's World, *Mississippi Noir,* and the print edition of *The Saturday Evening Post.* A former Air Force captain and IBM systems engineer, he is also an Edgar Award finalist, a Shamus Award winner, a six-time Derringer Award winner, a three-time Pushcart Prize nominee, and the 2018 recipient of the Short Mystery Fiction Society's lifetime achievement award. John's stories have been selected for inclusion in the 2015, 2018, and 2020 editions of *Best American Mystery Stories* and the 2021 and 2024 editions of *Best Mystery Stories of the Year,* and were listed in the Best Mystery series as "Other Distinguished Mysteries of the year/Honor Roll" in 2000, 2010, 2012, 2016, 2017, and 2022.

T. Fox Dunham lives in Lancaster, Pennsylvania with his wife, Allison. He's a cancer survivor, disabled author, modern bard, herbalist, baker and historian. His first book, The Street Martyr in production by Throughline Films. He's a well-published crime, horror and Sci-fi author and a member of the Horror Writers Association. Fox is proud to have also contributed to official Stargate canon with a story published in the Stargate Anthology Points of Origin from Fandemonium Books, telling the last story of the Asgard. He's edited one book of crime stories based on the music of Pink Floyd and co-edited a similar anthology based on the songs of Talking Heads. More information at tfoxdunham.com & Twitter: @TFoxDunham

Christine Verstraete is a Wisconsin author who enjoys writing mystery, horror, and whatever else she can dream up. Her stories have appeared in various publications including, *Noncorporeal II; Behind the Shadows II; (I Just) Died in Your Arms: Crime Fiction Inspired by One-Hit Wonders; The Creepy Podcast; Scare Street: Night Terrors. Vol. 26; The Colored Lens;, Mystery Weekly;* and others. She is the author of the *Lizzie Borden, Zombie Hunter* series. Learn more at her website, www.cverstraete.com and blogs https://candidcanine.blogspot.com, and https://girlzombieauthors.blogspot.com.

Shari Held is an award-winning fiction author and journalist who spins tales of mystery/crime, humor, romance, and fantasy. Her short stories have been published in more than three dozen magazines and anthologies, including *Hoosier Noir*, White Cat Publications, Yellow Mama, *Asinine Assassins*, and *Murder 20/20*, for which she served as co-editor. Shari also appears in the White City Press charity anthology *The Perp Wore* Pumpkin. She is a member of Sisters in Crime and the Short Mystery Fiction Society. When not writing, she cares for feral cats and other wildlife, attends movies, reads avidly, and enjoys watching tennis matches. Visit her website, www.shariheld.com, for more information about her and her stories.

www.ingramcontent.com/pod-product-compliance
Lightning Source LLC
Chambersburg PA
CBHW060317310726

48976CB00007B/2355